WRITTEN
SHOLLY F
DRAWN BY
CHRISTOPHER UMINGA
COLORED BY
SILVANA BRYS
LETTERED BY
DERON BENNETT
WITH
MORGAN MARTINEZ
BATMAN CREATED BY BOB KANE WITH BILL FINGER

BATMAN'S MYSTERY CASEBOOK

DC Comics, 2900 West Alameda Ave., Burbank, CA 91505

Printed by Worzalla, Stevens Point, WI, USA. 7/22/22
First Printing.
ISBN: 978-1-77950-586-6 JLG Edition ISBN: 978-1-77952-098-2

Library of Congress Cataloging-in-Publication Data

Names: Fisch, Sholly, writer. | Uminga, Christopher, artist. | Brys, Silvana, colourist. | Bennett, Deron, letterer. | Martinez, Morgan, letterer.
Title: Batman's mystery casebook / written by Sholly Fisch ; drawn by Christopher Uminga ; colored by Silvana Brys ;
lettered by Deron Bennett with Morgan Martinez.
Description: Burbank, CA : DC Comics, [2022] | "Batman created by Bob Kane with Bill Finger" | Audience: Ages 8-12 | Audience: Grades 4-6 |
Summary: Readers can help the great detective Batman and his sidekicks solve riddles, analyze evidence, look for clues,
and spot solutions to mysteries before he logs them into his casebook.
Identifiers: LCCN 2022010633 (print) | LCCN 2022010634 (ebook) | ISBN 9781779505866 (paperback) | ISBN 9781779508782 (ebook)
Subjects: CYAC: Graphic novels. | Superheroes--Fiction. | Mystery and detective stories. |
LCGFT: Graphic novels. | Detective and mystery fiction.
Classification: LCC PZ7.7.F57 Bat 2022 (print) | LCC PZ7.7.F57 (ebook) | DDC 741.5/973--dc23/eng/20220325
LC record available at https://lccn.loc.gov/2022010633
LC ebook record available at https://lccn.loc.gov/2022010634

MIX
Paper from responsible sources
FSC® C002589

BATMAN'S MYSTERY CASEBOOK

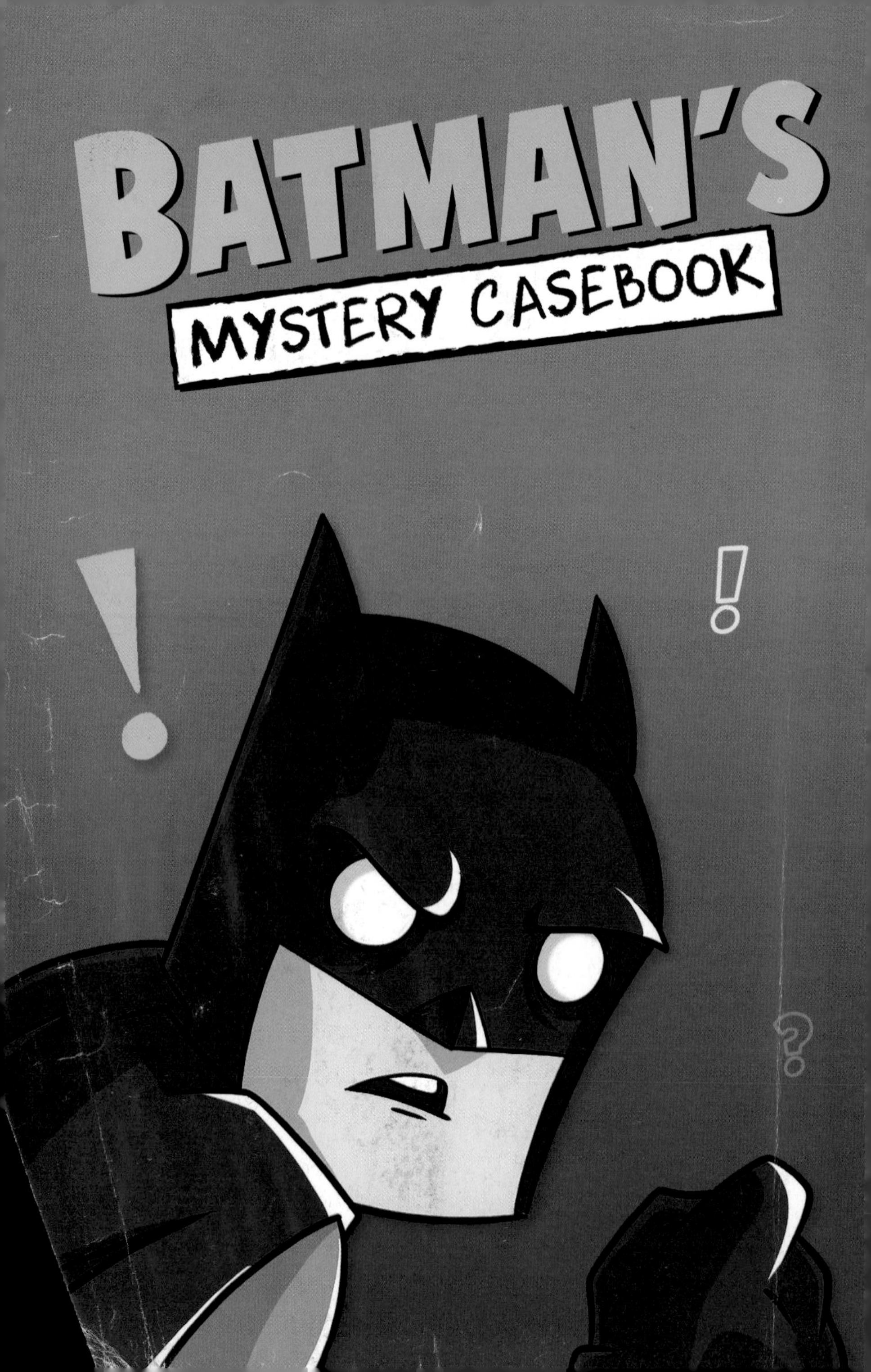
BATMAN'S
MYSTERY CASEBOOK

TABLE OF CONTENTS

PROLOGUE:
Whodunit?
Batman is the world's greatest detective. How good a detective are *you?*
This book will give you the chance to find out, as you try to crack some of our most puzzling cases. And you'll also learn all about forensic science, straight from the Batcave crime lab!
720

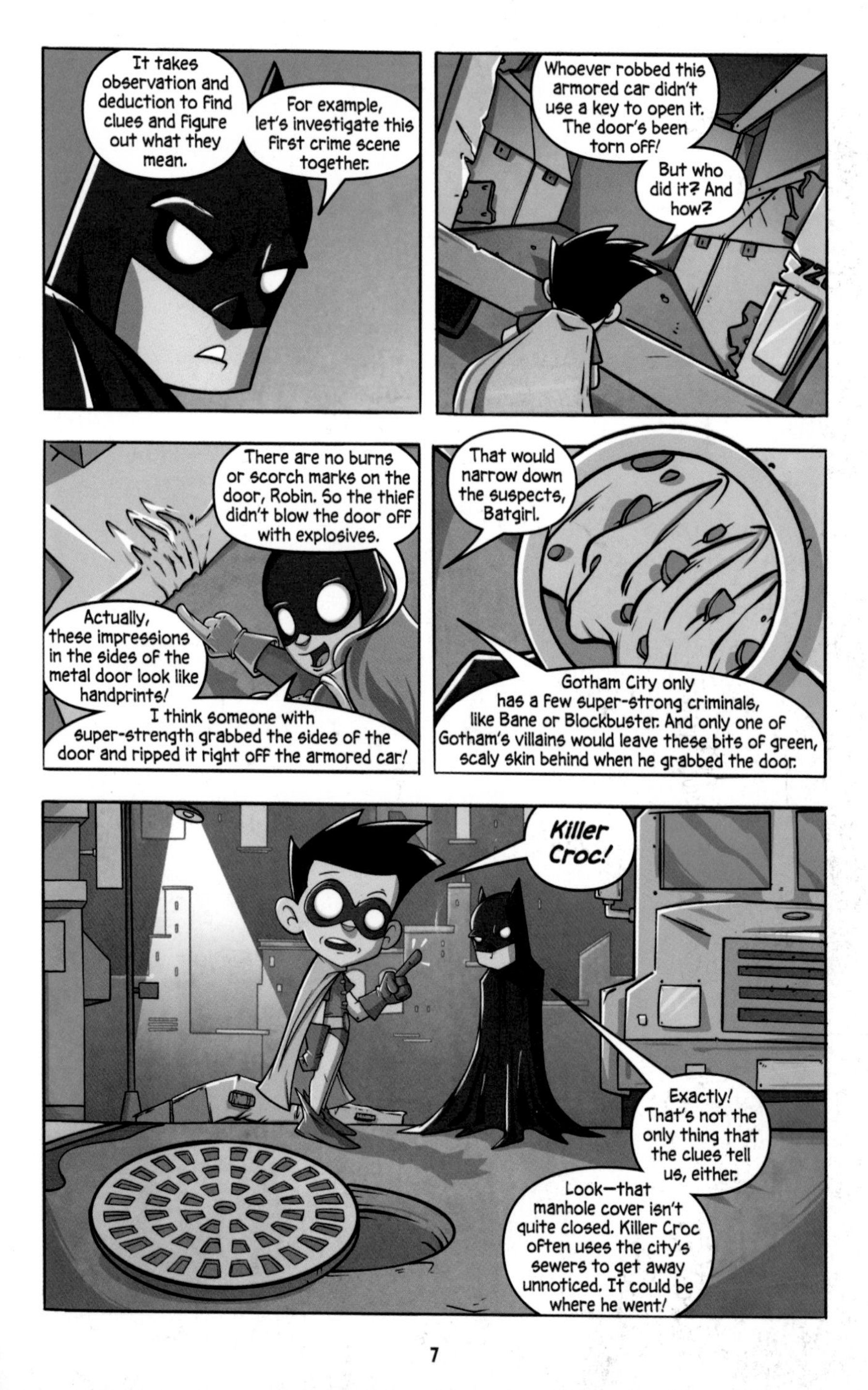
It takes observation and deduction to find clues and figure out what they mean.
For example, let's investigate this first crime scene together.
Whoever robbed this armored car didn't use a key to open it. The door's been torn off!
But who did it? And how?
There are no burns or scorch marks on the door, Robin. So the thief didn't blow the door off with explosives.
Actually, these impressions in the sides of the metal door look like handprints!
I think someone with super-strength grabbed the sides of the door and ripped it right off the armored car!
That would narrow down the suspects, Batgirl.
Gotham City only has a few super-strong criminals, like Bane or Blockbuster. And only one of Gotham's villains would leave these bits of green, scaly skin behind when he grabbed the door.
Killer Croc!
Exactly! That's not the only thing that the clues tell us, either.
Look—that manhole cover isn't quite closed. Killer Croc often uses the city's sewers to get away unnoticed. It could be where he went!

Got the hang of it now?
All of the mysteries in this book have clues in plain sight. But that doesn't mean the clues are easy to find!
Pay close attention and see if you can spot the clues before we do.
When you see this symbol, don't turn the page! Try to figure out the mystery first.
Then, when you think you've solved it, turn the page to reveal the answer and see if you're right.
Now, if you'll excuse us, I believe we've solved this mystery. It's time to move on to the next step...
Capturing the villain!
CASE CLOSED!

Robin.
Wake up.
Five more minutes...
Not this time. You're not at home.
Wh...what happened?
Knockout gas took us by surprise. I just woke up myself.
Apparently, while we were unconscious, we were brought here.
Where *is* "here"? The last thing I remember, we were fighting the Riddler.
You still are!

CHAPTER 1:
The Case of the Perilous Puzzles
Riddler! Why did you bring us here? You could have made a clean getaway while we were unconscious!
Where's the fun in that? It will be so much more satisfying to outwit you before you meet your end.
Welcome to my labyrinth—filled from end to end with death traps!

What makes you think we'll agree to play your twisted game?
You don't have a choice! You'll *have* to solve my riddles if you want to survive!
Can you answer the Riddler's riddles? Try to figure out what they mean in time to help Batman and Robin escape!
Ready, caped crusaders? You'd better be—because here's the first riddle...
How do you get down off an elephant?
I know that riddle. It's really old, although I'm not sure what the answer has to do with us.
"You don't get down off an elephant. You get down off a..."

DUCK!
Ha ha. I get it. "Get down off a duck."
"Down" like the feathers in a pillow.
Mm. And "duck" like "Duck down before the arrows hit you."
The Riddler isn't kidding around.

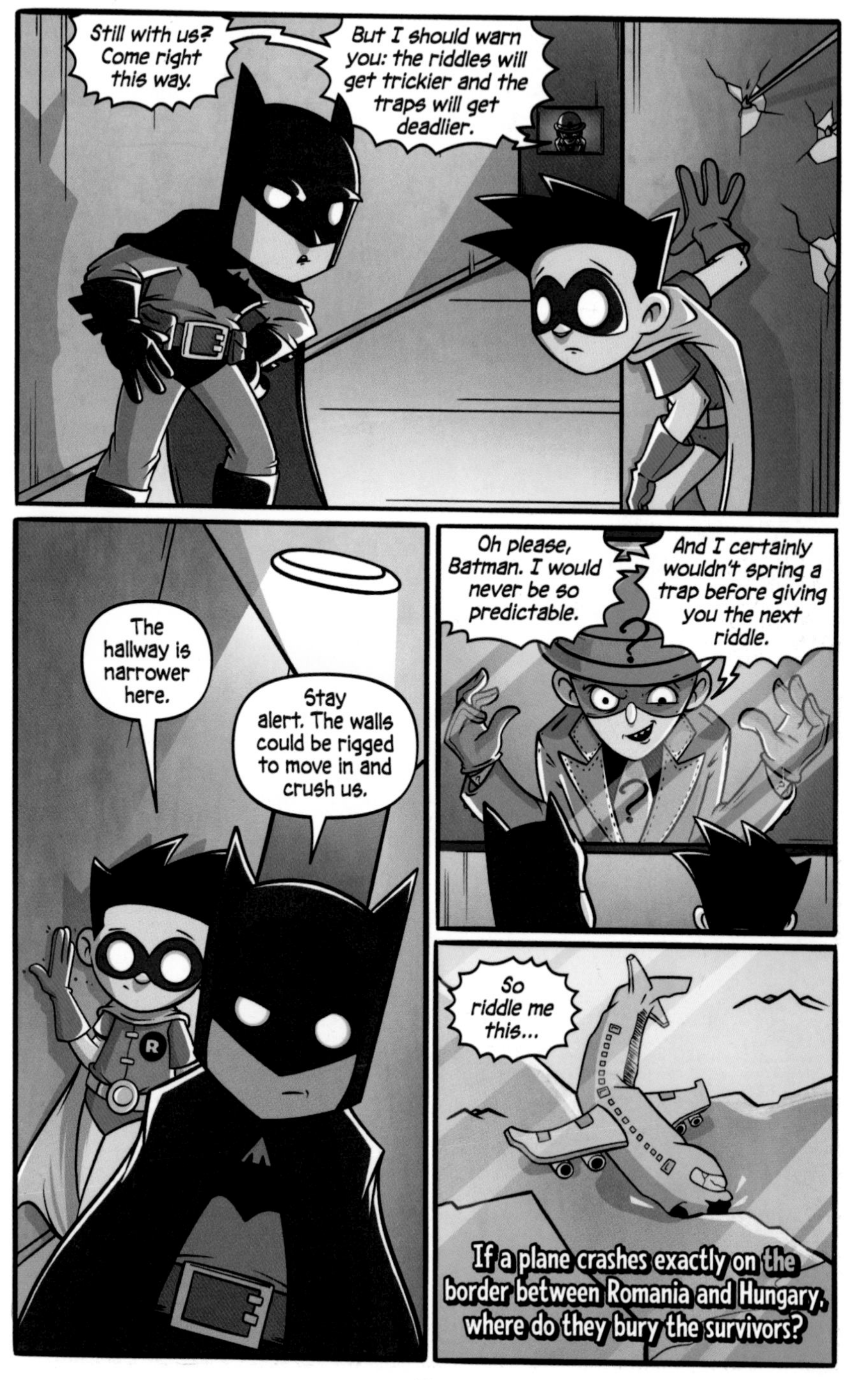

Still with us? Come right this way.
But I should warn you: the riddles will get trickier and the traps will get deadlier.
The hallway is narrower here.
Stay alert. The walls could be rigged to move in and crush us.
Oh please, Batman. I would never be so predictable.
And I certainly wouldn't spring a trap before giving you the next riddle.
So riddle me this...
If a plane crashes exactly on the border between Romania and Hungary, where do they bury the survivors?

Hmm...exactly on the border. Half and half?
Or maybe the answer has something to do with the countries in the riddle, Romania and Hungary...
Not necessarily...
The Riddler said his riddles would get "trickier." It's a trick question!
Of course! They wouldn't bury the survivors anywhere!
You don't bury survivors!
The walls— opening!
The Riddler's letting us out?

Or he's letting something *in!*
That's molten lava!
Jump!
Whew! ***We'd*** be buried under that lava if we were still down there—and we wouldn't be survivors!

We're not out of this yet. Molten lava is hotter than 1,000 degrees Fahrenheit. We can't drop down to the floor.
We can't keep holding ourselves up here forever, either! After a while, our muscles will get tired.
Cough Not to mention that the *cough* fumes from the lava make it hard to breathe!
If we can't stay here and we can't get down, then how do we get out?
Slowly and carefully.
Keep bracing your arms and legs against the wall. Inch them forward, little by little.
It won't be easy, but we can creep along the wall until we're past the lava.

No lava in *this* hallway!
But the *Riddler's* here. I'm not sure which is worse.
Sticks and stones, Boy Wonder. But my next riddle may hurt you!
Hmmm... I wonder what these are for...
Don't tell me the Riddler wants us to bake a cake...
The only thing I've cooked up is another riddle!
You have a four-cup measure, an eight-ounce glass, and a teaspoon. What's the quickest way to drain a forty-gallon barrel?

Well, the measuring cup is biggest, so using it would be the fastest way to drain the barrel. Seems pretty obvious.

Too obvious! Actually, there's a quicker way to drain the barrel.

What's that?

Kick it over!

SHZZAAAKKTTT

Whoa! That barrel isn't full of water!

It's full of laser blasters!

Yes, but tipping over the barrel pointed the lasers up at the ceiling, instead of at us.

We should be safe until we move on to the next hallway.

Or not!
Fortunately, Robin and I are strong swimmers.
But that barrel is still floating on the surface—and firing lasers!
Robin—dive down!

That was close! As long as that barrel's bobbing in the water, we'll have to time our motion to avoid the lasers.
I thought you wanted to outwit us, Riddler! A pit of water isn't very imaginative.
There's not even a riddle with a clue about how to escape!
Oh, I already gave you the riddle, Batman. You just weren't bold enough to see it!
And if you want something more creative...

That Flamethrower is too dangerous! With the scuba masks from our utility belts, we'll be safer down here.
Until the air supply in our masks runs out, at least. After that, we won't be able to surface and take a breath.
Then I guess we'll have to solve the Riddler's puzzle before then.
What puzzle?
The Riddler said we weren't bold enough to see his riddle, but where was it? Under the lava? Inside the barrel of lasers?
No, I think the Riddler's puzzle was right in front of us. If I'm right, I believe I've figured out the answer too!
STOP!
DON'T TURN THE PAGE!
Did you spot the puzzle? How can it help Batman and Robin escape?
Take another look. Then, when you're ready, turn the page to see if you're right.

The puzzle was in plain sight? Where?
In plain sight, all the time.
It caught my eye, but I didn't pay attention to it at the time.
Careful. Lasers.
The Riddler kept **talking** to us, but he gave us all of his riddles in **writing.** Why?
get down off an
on the border
way to drain a
In each riddle, one word was printed in bold. The choice of bold words seemed random...
Until the Riddler said we'd have to be "**bold** enough" to see the riddle!
I get it! When you put the three bold words **together,** they say...
"Down the drain."

Since flames and lasers are "up," "down" sounds good to me!
ƸNnmghƷ If we can get this grate off, that is! We'll need tools from our utility belts.
Or you can just swim away to the side, and...
SHZZAAAKKTTT
The Riddler didn't realize how considerate it was to give us these lasers. So much for the grate!
SHZZAAAKKTTT
And that takes care of the flame-thrower too!
Nice! Then we have a choice. Should we take the high road or the low road?
Actually, with this laser, we can carve out our **own** road.

Impossible! They're not in the pit, and I don't see them in the drainpipe either!
Where could they have gone?
Good question. Here's one for *you.*
Wha—?
SHZZAAAKKTT
Usually, filling a barrel makes it heavier. What fills a barrel to make it lighter?
Answer— *light!*
Like, say, a laser!
We used your lasers to cut a way out of the labyrinth and locate your hiding place.
Looks like we've seen our last riddle for a while.
Well, maybe just one *more*— why is the Riddler like a fly ball?
Yeah, I know.
We both get caught.
CASE CLOSED!

The Batcave Crime Lab: Crime Scene Investigation
There's more to crime-fighting than just battling super-powered menaces like ClayFace.
It takes *evidence* to solve crimes and identify who's responsible. Later, that evidence also supplies proof to send the criminals to prison.
Witnesses provide some evidence by telling what they've seen. Other types of evidence are physical — objects or traces that detectives find at the scene of a crime, or with someone they suspect was involved.
The science of finding and analyzing physical evidence is called *"Forensics."* That's what we do here in the Batcave's crime lab.

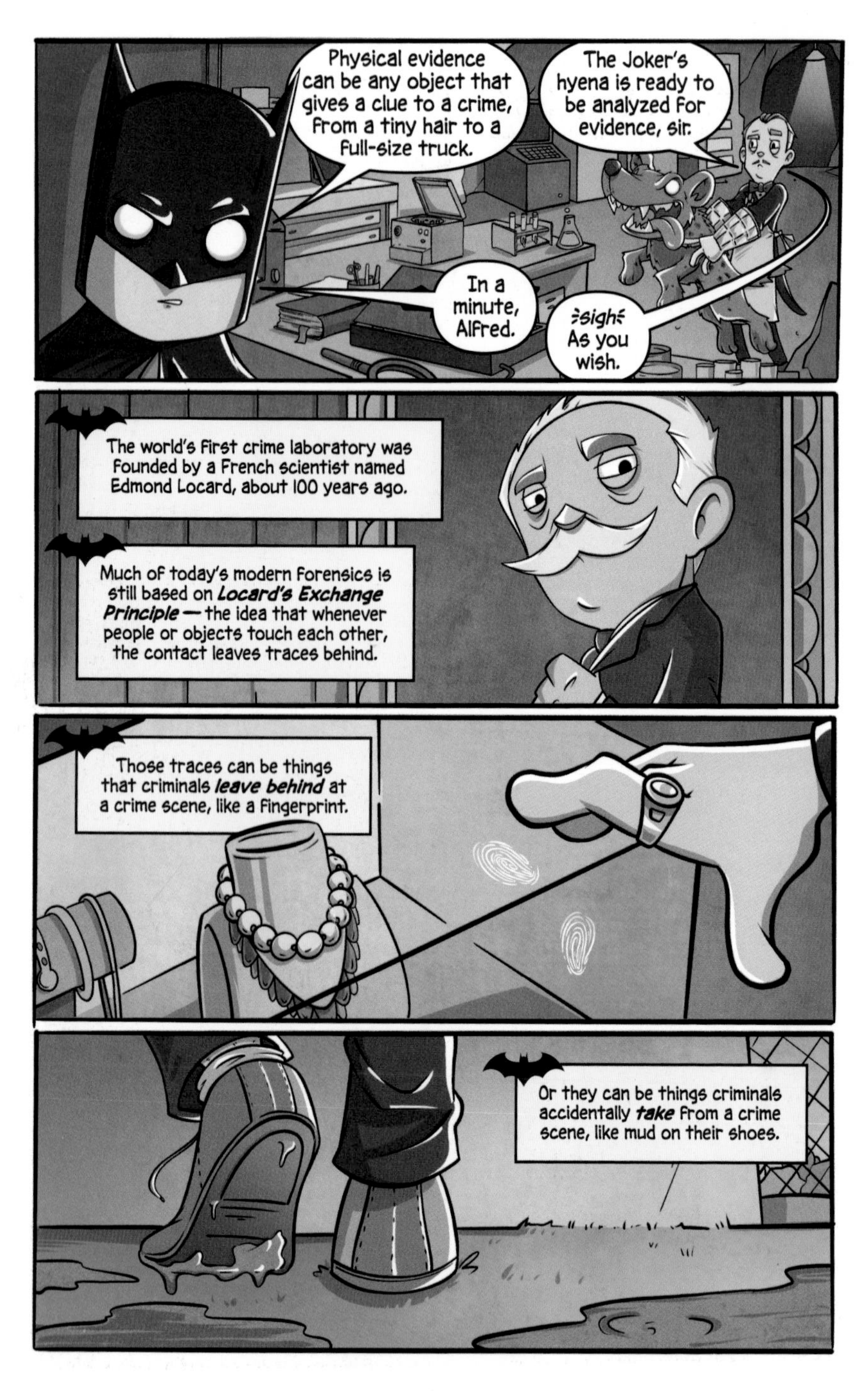
Physical evidence can be any object that gives a clue to a crime, from a tiny hair to a full-size truck.
The Joker's hyena is ready to be analyzed for evidence, sir.
In a minute, Alfred.
sigh As you wish.
The world's first crime laboratory was founded by a French scientist named Edmond Locard, about 100 years ago.
Much of today's modern forensics is still based on *Locard's Exchange Principle* — the idea that whenever people or objects touch each other, the contact leaves traces behind.
Those traces can be things that criminals *leave behind* at a crime scene, like a fingerprint.
Or they can be things criminals accidentally *take* from a crime scene, like mud on their shoes.

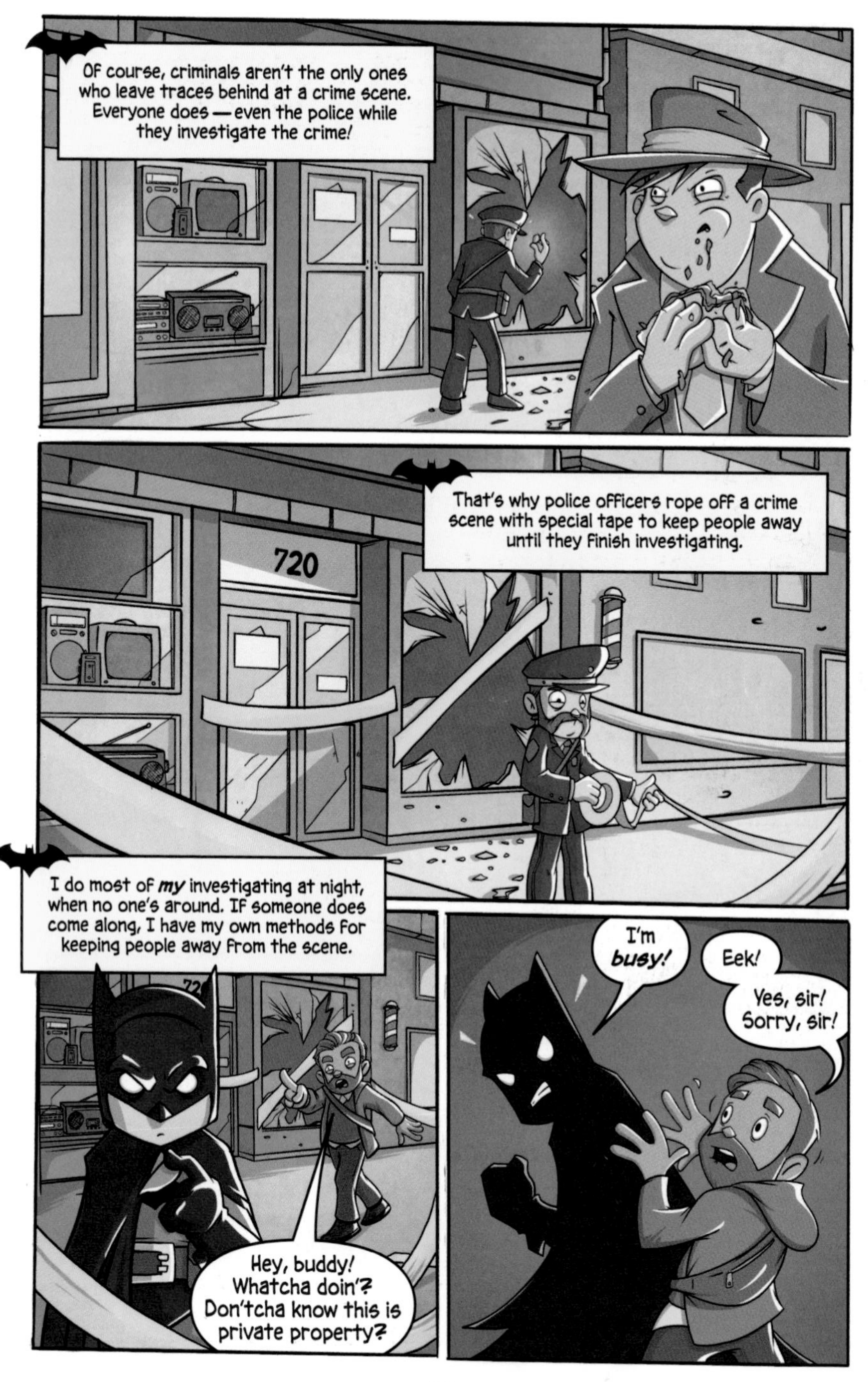
Of course, criminals aren't the only ones who leave traces behind at a crime scene. Everyone does — even the police while they investigate the crime!
That's why police officers rope off a crime scene with special tape to keep people away until they finish investigating.
720
I do most of *my* investigating at night, when no one's around. If someone does come along, I have my own methods for keeping people away from the scene.
Hey, buddy! Whatcha doin'? Don'tcha know this is private property?
I'm *busy!*
Eek!
Yes, sir! Sorry, sir!

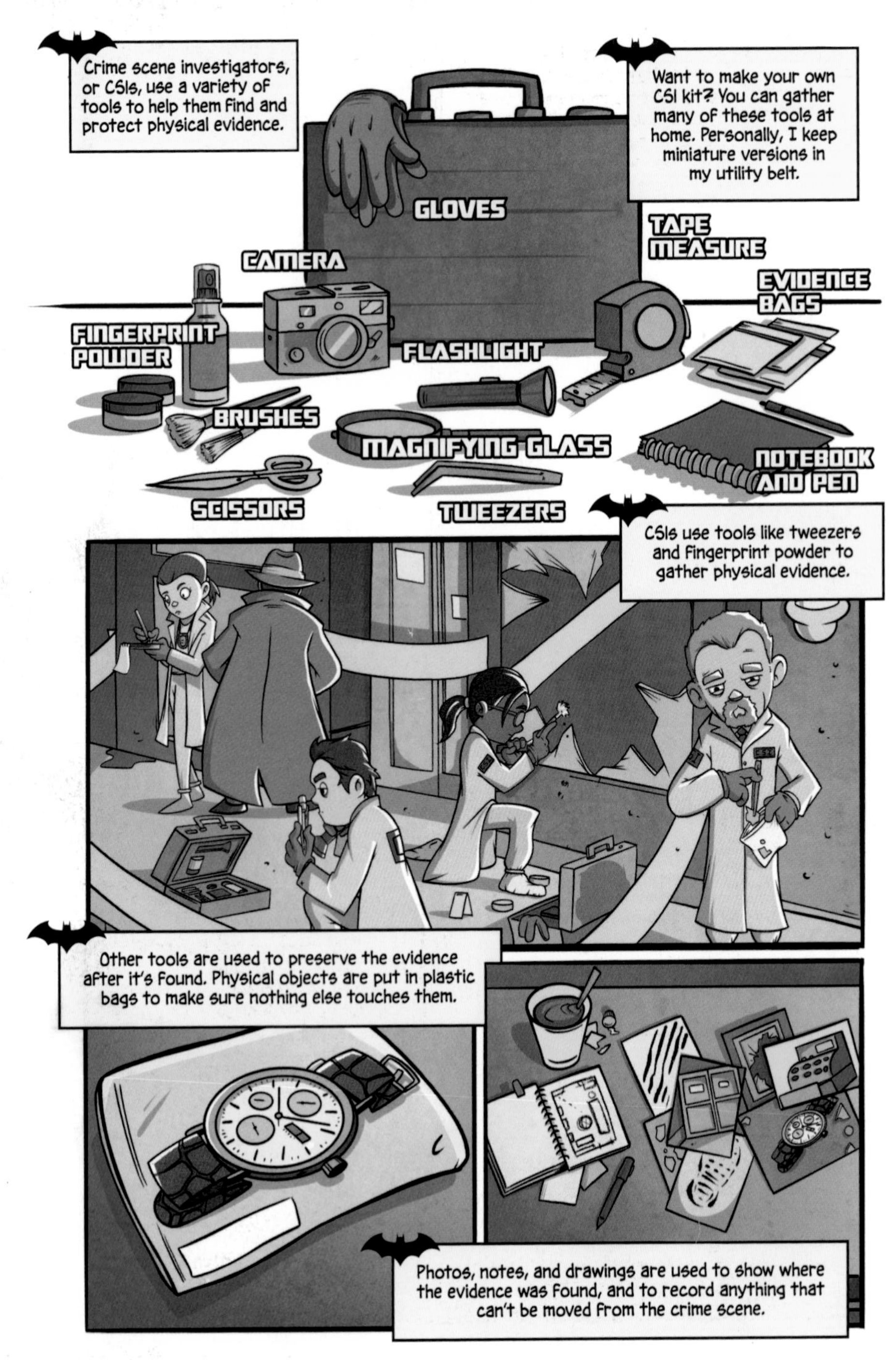
Crime scene investigators, or CSIs, use a variety of tools to help them find and protect physical evidence.
Want to make your own CSI kit? You can gather many of these tools at home. Personally, I keep miniature versions in my utility belt.
GLOVES
TAPE MEASURE
CAMERA
EVIDENCE BAGS
FINGERPRINT POWDER
FLASHLIGHT
BRUSHES
MAGNIFYING GLASS
NOTEBOOK AND PEN
SCISSORS
TWEEZERS
CSIs use tools like tweezers and fingerprint powder to gather physical evidence.
Other tools are used to preserve the evidence after it's found. Physical objects are put in plastic bags to make sure nothing else touches them.
Photos, notes, and drawings are used to show where the evidence was found, and to record anything that can't be moved from the crime scene.

Yet, even after detectives find clues, they still have to figure out what those clues mean. Detectives have to put all of the pieces together so that the evidence can tell its story.
That requires a detective's *greatest* tool...
...their *minds.*
Speaking of minds, sir...
Would you *mind* examining the hyena now?
Yes, thank you, Alfred. Hold it still while I search its fur for clues.
SNARL
SNORT
Nothing would make me happier.
CASE CLOSED!

Two-Face is obsessed with the number two.
I won't say it a *second* time!
With that in mind, it wasn't hard to predict that he'd try to steal a priceless collection of rare Spanish *doubl*oons.
Don't try to stop me...
CHAPTER 2:
The Case of the Dual Identity
I wasn't expecting him to dress as a pirate, though.
Or my henchmen will cut these tourists in two!

gulp
W-why'd we come to Gotham City for our vacation? We could've been swimming in Hawaii!
Lucky for you, my two-headed coin landed good side up...
So, I'll grant your wish. Happy swimming!
No!
Helllp!
Come on, Robin! We've got to save them!
Ha! Even Batman and Robin can't be in two places at once!
Stay calm, everyone. We've got you.
Good thing my cape is drip-dry.

Is everyone all right?
I...think so, thanks to you two.
But those crooks are getting away!
That's why Two-Face pushed you overboard.
He knew we'd be too busy saving you to stop them.
But they won't get away for long!
Sorry your vacations got spoiled!
Spoiled? Are you kidding?
Nobody back home in Boise'll believe we were rescued by Batman and Robin!
Aw, man! I forgot to take a selfie!

I saw which direction Two-Face went, but he and his gang have a big head start. It'll be hard to follow them.
That's why I'm using my palmtop computer to hack into Gotham's traffic camera system. If one of the cameras caught an image of their getaway car...
Found them! They drove north on Robinson Avenue, two minutes ago.
VRROOOOOOMMMMM
I'll check the cameras farther down Robinson and see if I can find where they turned next.

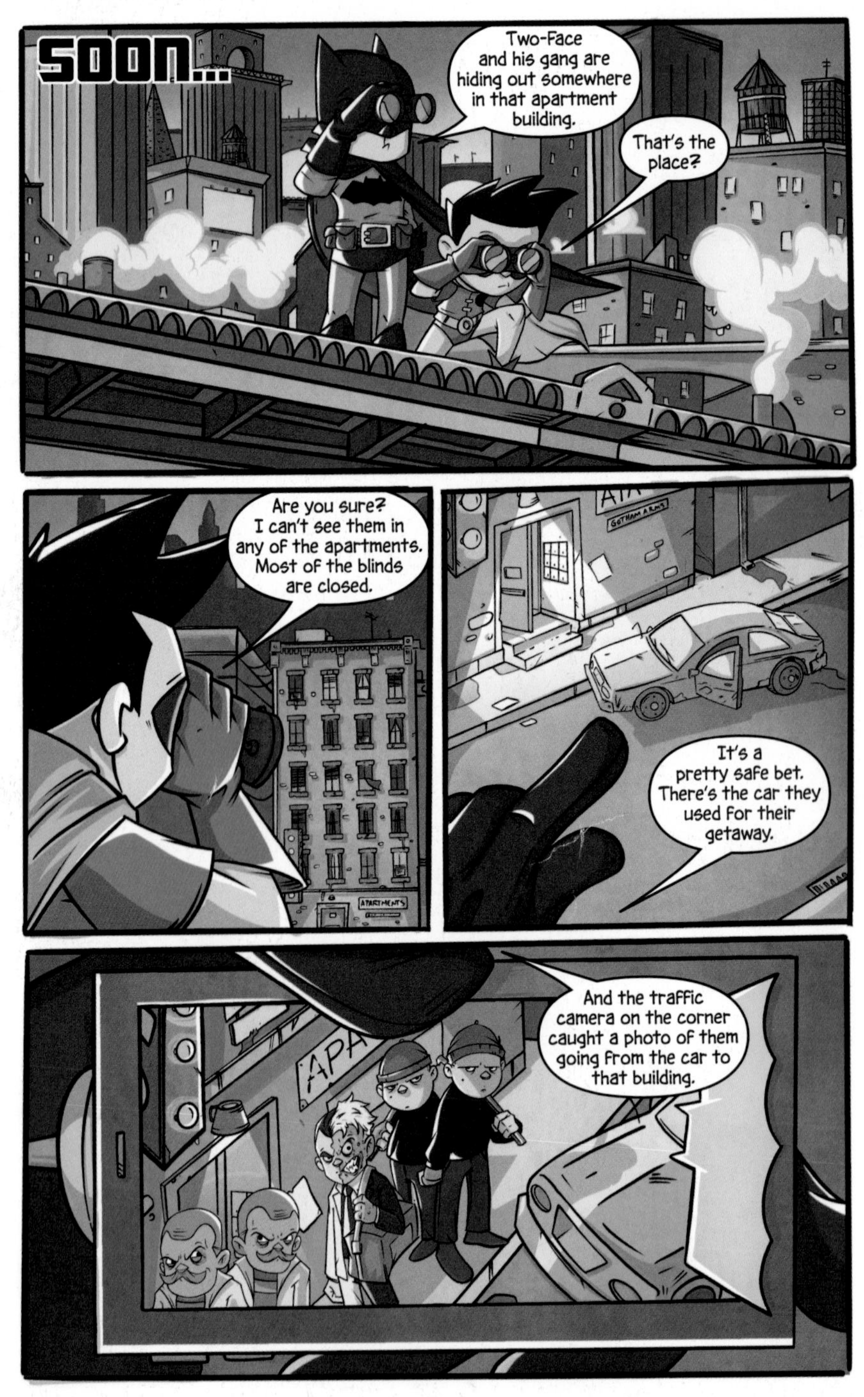
SOON...
Two-Face and his gang are hiding out somewhere in that apartment building.
That's the place?
Are you sure? I can't see them in any of the apartments. Most of the blinds are closed.
APARTMENTS
GOTHAM ARMS
It's a pretty safe bet. There's the car they used for their getaway.
And the traffic camera on the corner caught a photo of them going from the car to that building.

Then what are we waiting for? Let's go get them!
Not so fast.
I count ten apartments in that building, and we don't know which one they're in.
If we pick the wrong one, the commotion will alert Two-Face and he'll escape.
Well, isn't it obvious? Two-Face must be in apartment number 2! Or one of the apartments on the second floor!
Maybe...
But we have to be certain.
I'm pulling up the building records on my computer, to see who's renting those apartments.
That might give us the answer.

Got it! Here are the names.

Apt. 1
Alvin Schmidt

Apt. 2
Sanford Hausler

Apt. 3
Marcie Benoit

Apt. 4
D. Feldman

Apt. 5
M. Geller/R. Green

Apt. 6
Paolo Dominguez

Apt. 7
Lee Shen

Apt. 8
B. Jonas

Apt. 9
J. Fry/K. Nijuck

Apt. 10
Janus Bartlett

Okay, but I don't see Two-Face's real name, Harvey Dent, on the list.
I'd be surprised if it was.
Two-Face wouldn't rent an apartment under his real name.
He'd use an alias.
Then, *any* of those names could be Two-Face's alias!
Which apartment is his hideout?
I think I know...
DON'T TURN THE PAGE!
STOP!
?
Do you know which apartment is Two-Face's hideout? Take another look at the clues and try to figure it out.
When you think you have the answer, turn the page to see if you're right.

Batman and Robin!
You were right, Batman!
How'd you know to check *Janus Bartlett's* apartment?
The key was the way "Janus" was spelled.
"Janice" is a common name in today's world, but "Janus" is a figure from Roman mythology.
The ancient Janus looked to the past and the future—
— with two faces!
And "Bartlett"?
You'll find that answer in the produce aisle at the supermarket. Bartlett is a species of pear...or, as Two-Face would say, "pair"!
That made the name a ***double*** pun!

And I guess that's the *punch* line!
But it's not half as painful as that joke.
I still don't get why Two-Face would rent apartment 10, though. Shouldn't he have chosen apartment 2?
In a sense, he *did.*
You and I write numbers like this. Zero, one, two.
0 = 00
But computers represent numbers differently, using the binary system. This is how to write the numbers 0 and 1 in binary code.
00
= 01
And this is how you write the number 2!
Is it any wonder that Two-Face chose his apartment number in *bi*-nary?
0 = 00
1 = 01
2 = 10
CASE CLOSED!

Batcave
Crime Lab:
Fingerprints
Fingerprints are such an important tool in identifying criminals that it's hard to imagine fighting crime without them.
Actually, though, detectives only started using fingerprints less than 150 years ago.
"You probably know why fingerprints are so useful to detectives.
"Everyone's fingerprints are different.
"But did you know that not even identical twins have identical fingerprints?

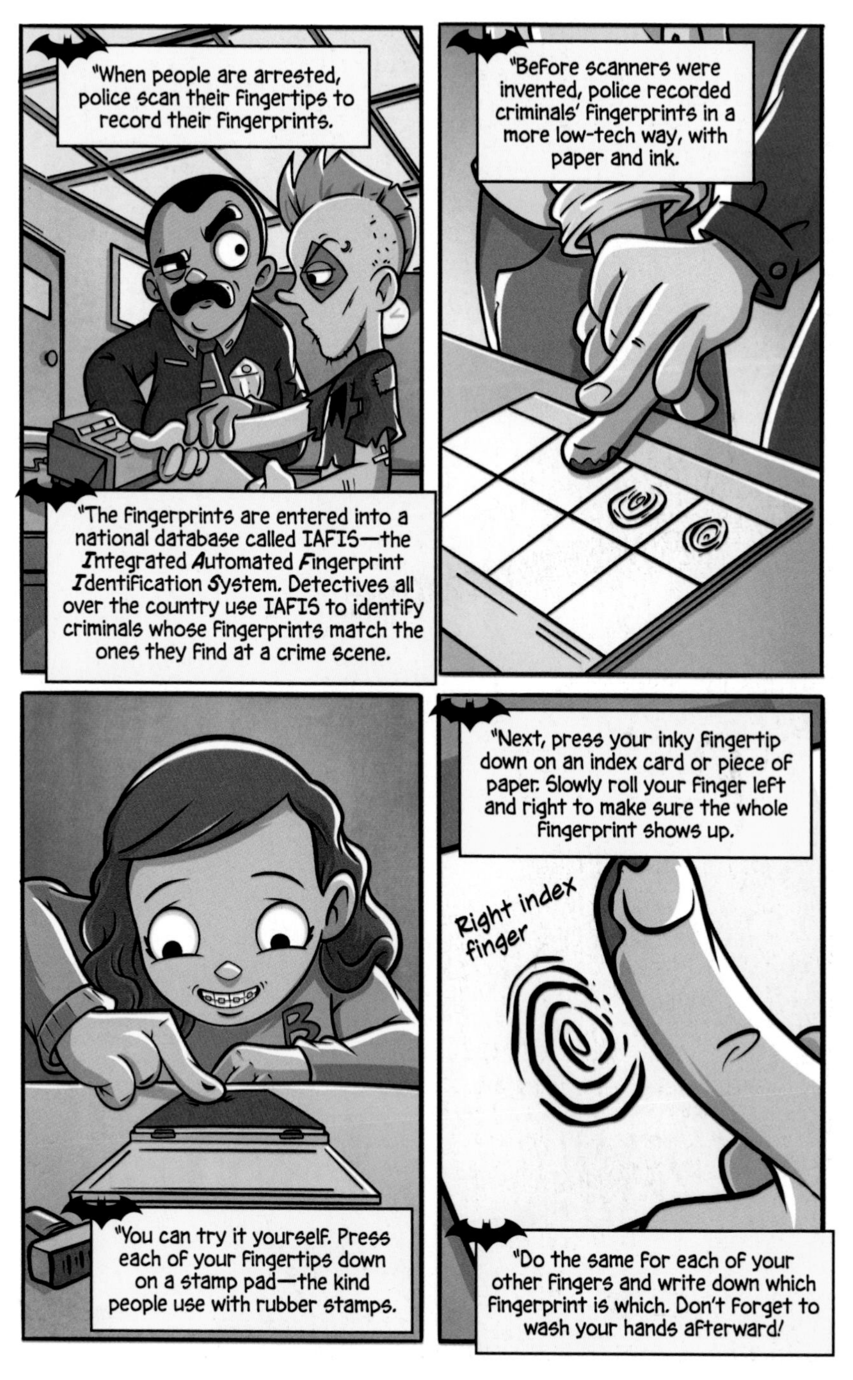
"When people are arrested, police scan their fingertips to record their fingerprints.
"The fingerprints are entered into a national database called IAFIS—the Integrated Automated Fingerprint Identification System. Detectives all over the country use IAFIS to identify criminals whose fingerprints match the ones they find at a crime scene.
"Before scanners were invented, police recorded criminals' fingerprints in a more low-tech way, with paper and ink.
"You can try it yourself. Press each of your fingertips down on a stamp pad—the kind people use with rubber stamps.
"Next, press your inky fingertip down on an index card or piece of paper. Slowly roll your finger left and right to make sure the whole fingerprint shows up.
Right index finger
"Do the same for each of your other fingers and write down which fingerprint is which. Don't forget to wash your hands afterward!

WHORL
ARCH
TENTARCH
RIGHT LOOP
LEFT LOOP
DOUBLE LOOP
Fingerprints are classified by their patterns.
Here are some of the basic types of fingerprints. Which ones are most like yours?

"If you've ever made a mess with chocolatey hands, you've seen that some fingerprints are visible. Detectives call those 'patent prints.'
"But, even when you can't see fingerprints, it doesn't mean they're not there.
"The oil from your skin leaves invisible 'latent prints' on just about everything you touch.
"To make latent prints visible, detectives 'dust' fingerprints with a light coating of powder. The powder sticks to the print so that it can be seen."
Sometimes, instead of powder, detectives use chemical fumes. They stick to fingerprints and make them visible, too.

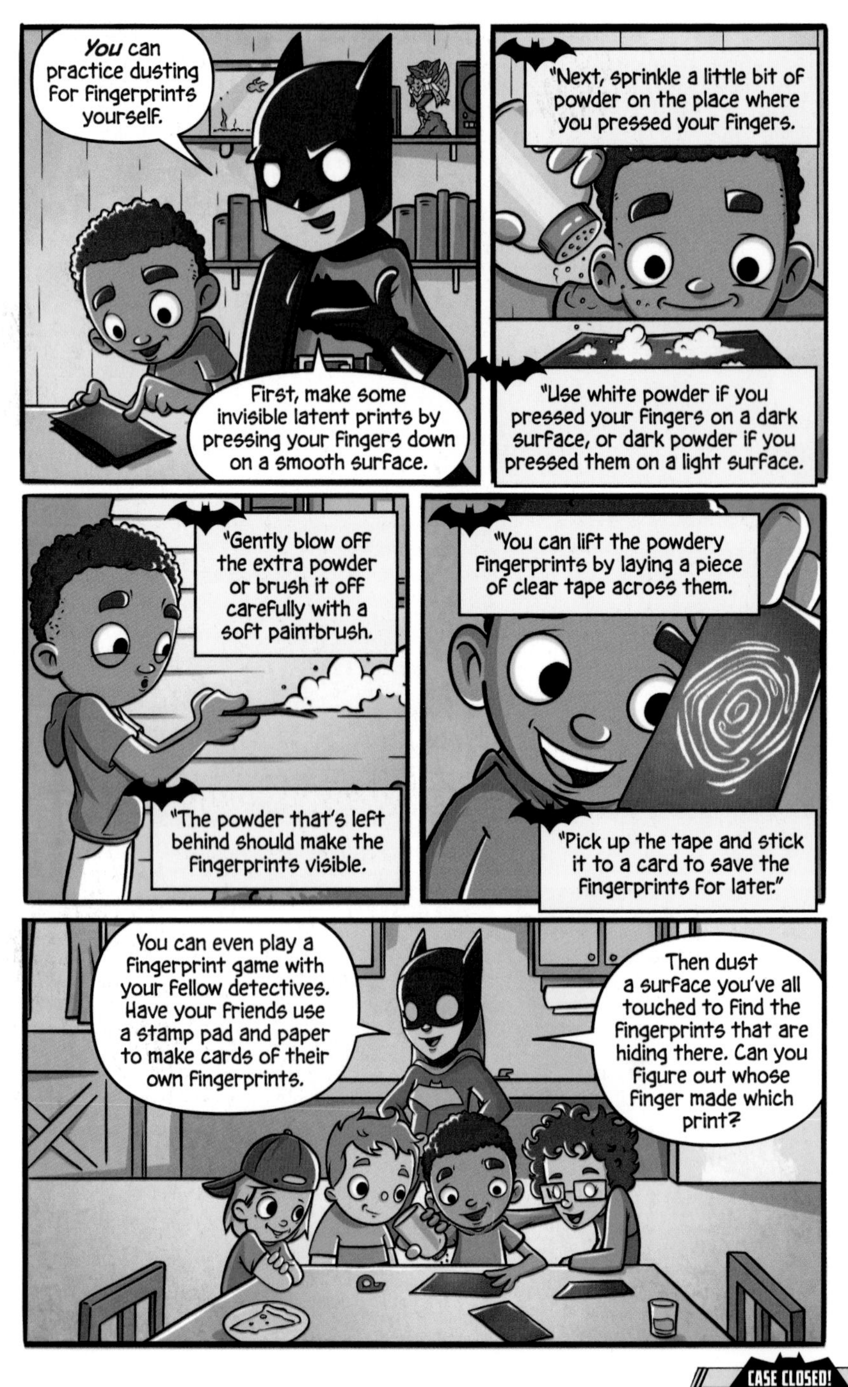
You can practice dusting for fingerprints yourself.
First, make some invisible latent prints by pressing your fingers down on a smooth surface.
"Next, sprinkle a little bit of powder on the place where you pressed your fingers.
"Use white powder if you pressed your fingers on a dark surface, or dark powder if you pressed them on a light surface.
"Gently blow off the extra powder or brush it off carefully with a soft paintbrush.
"The powder that's left behind should make the fingerprints visible.
"You can lift the powdery fingerprints by laying a piece of clear tape across them.
"Pick up the tape and stick it to a card to save the fingerprints for later."
You can even play a fingerprint game with your fellow detectives. Have your friends use a stamp pad and paper to make cards of their own fingerprints.
Then dust a surface you've all touched to find the fingerprints that are hiding there. Can you figure out whose finger made which print?
CASE CLOSED!

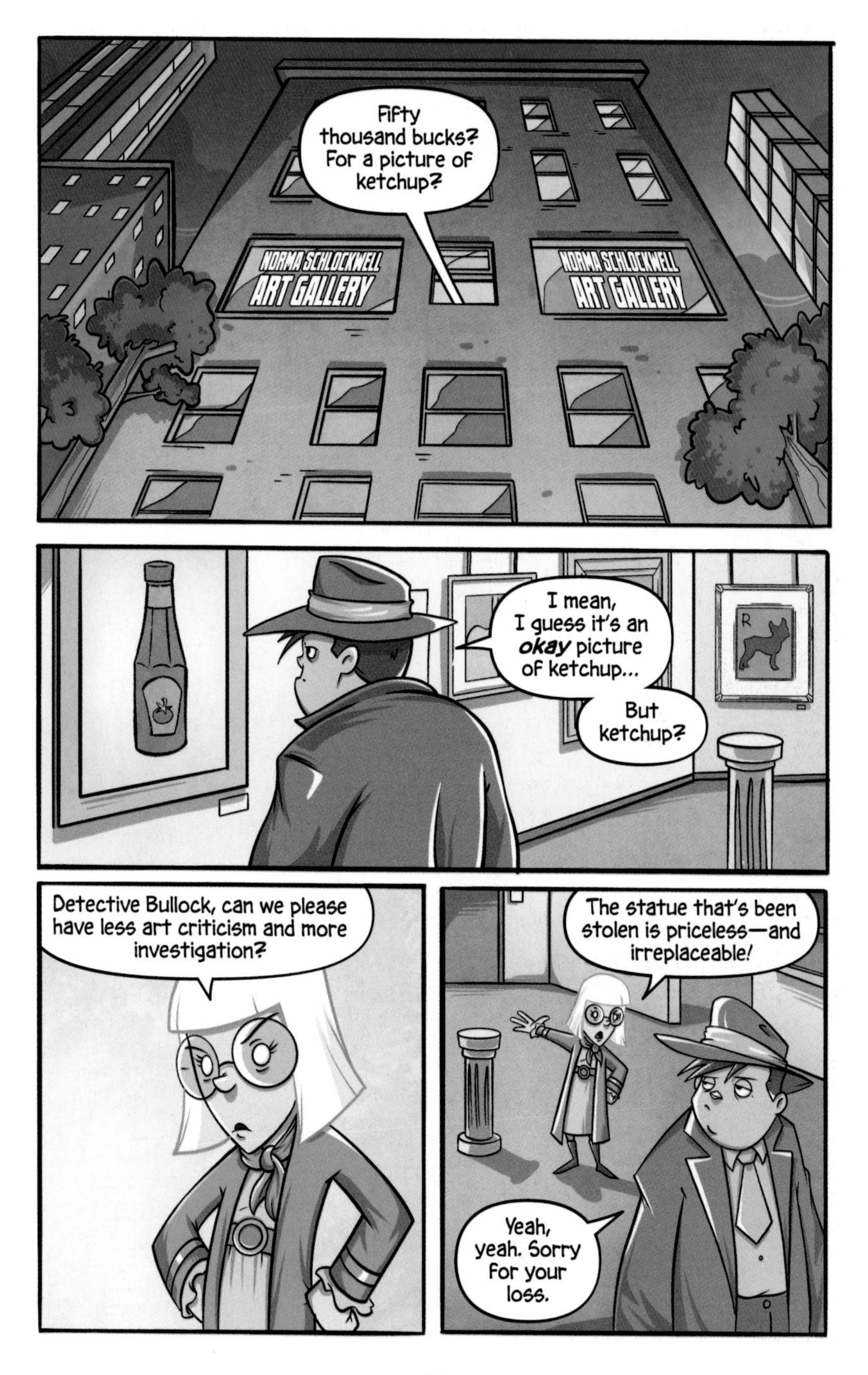
Fifty thousand bucks? For a picture of ketchup?
NORMA SCHLOCKWELL ART GALLERY
NORMA SCHLOCKWELL ART GALLERY
I mean, I guess it's an *okay* picture of ketchup...
But ketchup?
Detective Bullock, can we please have less art criticism and more investigation?
The statue that's been stolen is priceless—and irreplaceable!
Yeah, yeah. Sorry for your loss.

CHAPTER 3:
The Case of the
Art Attack
Maybe you'd better tell us what happened from the beginning, Ms. Schlockwell.

Hey! Leave the police work to the professionals, kid!
Commissioner Gordon might say I have to put up with you bat-weirdoes, but that doesn't mean I've gotta *like* it!
Maybe not. But I'm not going anywhere, so you'd better get used to it!
Wait a minute...why does this feel so familiar?
Um...
Uh-oh. I have to be more careful.
Harvey Bullock works with my dad, Commissioner Gordon—and he's met me plenty of times in my secret identity.
What do you mean, police stations are no place for Take Your Child to Work Day?
I'm not going anywhere, so you'd better get used to it!
If I don't want him to figure out I'm *Barbara Gordon*, I'd better change the subject.
Um, let's focus on investigating the robbery. Why don't you show me how the professionals do it?
Watch and learn.
So, lady, why don'tcha tell us what happened from the beginning?
Wow, wish *I'd* thought of that.

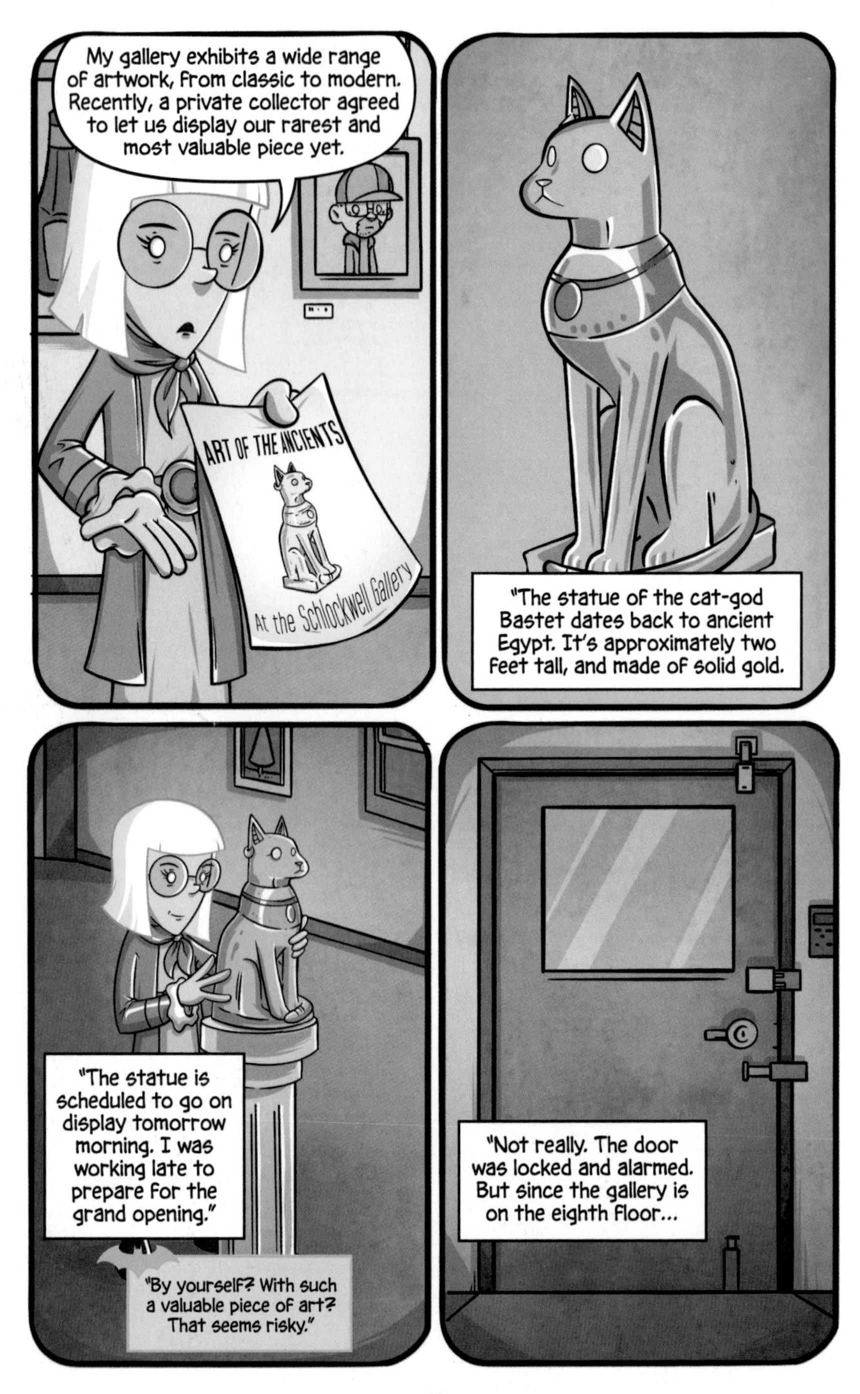
My gallery exhibits a wide range of artwork, from classic to modern. Recently, a private collector agreed to let us display our rarest and most valuable piece yet.
ART OF THE ANCIENTS
At the Schlockwell Gallery
"The statue of the cat-god Bastet dates back to ancient Egypt. It's approximately two feet tall, and made of solid gold.
"The statue is scheduled to go on display tomorrow morning. I was working late to prepare for the grand opening."
"By yourself? With such a valuable piece of art? That seems risky."
"Not really. The door was locked and alarmed. But since the gallery is on the eighth floor...

"It didn't occur to me that anyone could possibly come in through the window.
"I never even saw the thief, until it was too late.
"Before I knew it...
"I was trapped—by *Catwoman!*"

Mmf! Mmmf!
Hmm? What's that you say?
Were you saying that I can have this?
Mmmff! Mmf! Mmf!
My, how kind!
Mm, and heavy.
This will be a lovely addition to my *cat*acombs.

"My only hope was that, with both hands full, Catwoman couldn't leap back out the window. She'd have to open the door, which would set off the burglar alarm.
"Then, downstairs, the building's doorman could stop her from escaping—or at least call the police.
"That's what I *thought,* anyway. But, instead, she did the one thing I never expected her to do.
"She threw the statue out an eighth-floor window!

"The statue of Bastet was a 3000-year-old artifact. Why would Catwoman smash it to bits on the street below?"
MMMMMFFF!
"But I was wrong. She wasn't destroying the statue.
"She was throwing it to her henchman on the roof across the street!
"After that, Catwoman leaped out the window and disappeared into the night.
"That's the last I saw of her...or the statue.

"It took me hours to wriggle out of the ropes and get free.
"I called the police right away. But, by then, Catwoman was long gone."
Jumpin' out an eighth-floor window, huh? That's some getaway.
It sure **sounds** like Catwoman, though.
There are still a few hours left before the gallery opens for the day. You **have** to help me get the statue back before then!
If anyone finds out that we lost the Bastet statue, the gallery will be finished!

"Finished"? Don't you guys have insurance in case anything gets stolen?
For the statue's *monetary* value, sure. I already sent a message to our insurance company. They'll pay for the statue if we don't get it back.
But there's a much greater loss here.
She means the *historical* loss. An ancient artifact like this would be irreplaceable!
Not to mention that, once word gets out, no one will ever want to trust us with their art again!
The gallery will have to close down and go out of business!
Well, don't worry about that yet.
"Yet"?
We'll do everything we can to recover your kitty.

Headquarters, this is Detective Bullock! Put out an all-points bulletin on Catwoman! You know the description— black suit, pointy ears...
Hold on! You can cancel that all-points bulletin.
Oh really? How come?
Because this crime *wasn't* committed by Catwoman!
STOP!
DON'T TURN THE PAGE!
?
What does Batgirl mean? If Catwoman's not guilty, who is?
Check back over the clues. When you think you've figured it out, turn the page to see if you're right.

Shyeah, right. If you don't think Catwoman took the statue, who did?
Simple...
Nobody!
What? That's ridiculous!
Do you *see* the statue anywhere around here? I just told you what happened!
True. You *told* us that Catwoman stole the statue and threw it across the street to her henchman.
"But the thing is, gold is very heavy. A solid gold statue that size would weigh hundreds of pounds.
"You'd need super-strength to even *lift* a statue that heavy, let alone throw it across a street!
"And Catwoman doesn't have super-strength.

You would have known how much it weighs if you really had the statue. I doubt the statue was *ever* here...assuming it really exists at all!
Interesting?
Especially since you already claimed money from your insurance company for the statue that got "stolen."
Sounds like somebody needs to be arrested for fraud!
I... I...
How disappointing. After all the advertising, I was so looking forward to getting up close with the Bastet statue myself.
And now, I find it isn't even real.
Catwoman! For real, this time!
I don't care that you tried to cheat your insurance company. But you tried to frame *me!*
So it seems only fair that I steal something from *you!* Since there's no Bastet statue, I suppose I'll take this instead!
After all, it *is* a fifty-thousand dollar painting of *cat*sup!
Oh, and thanks for clearing my not-so-good name, Batgirl.
No problem. When I catch you, Ms. Schlockwell can share your jail cell!
You have the right to remain silent...
Sigh What could I possibly say?

CASE CLOSED!

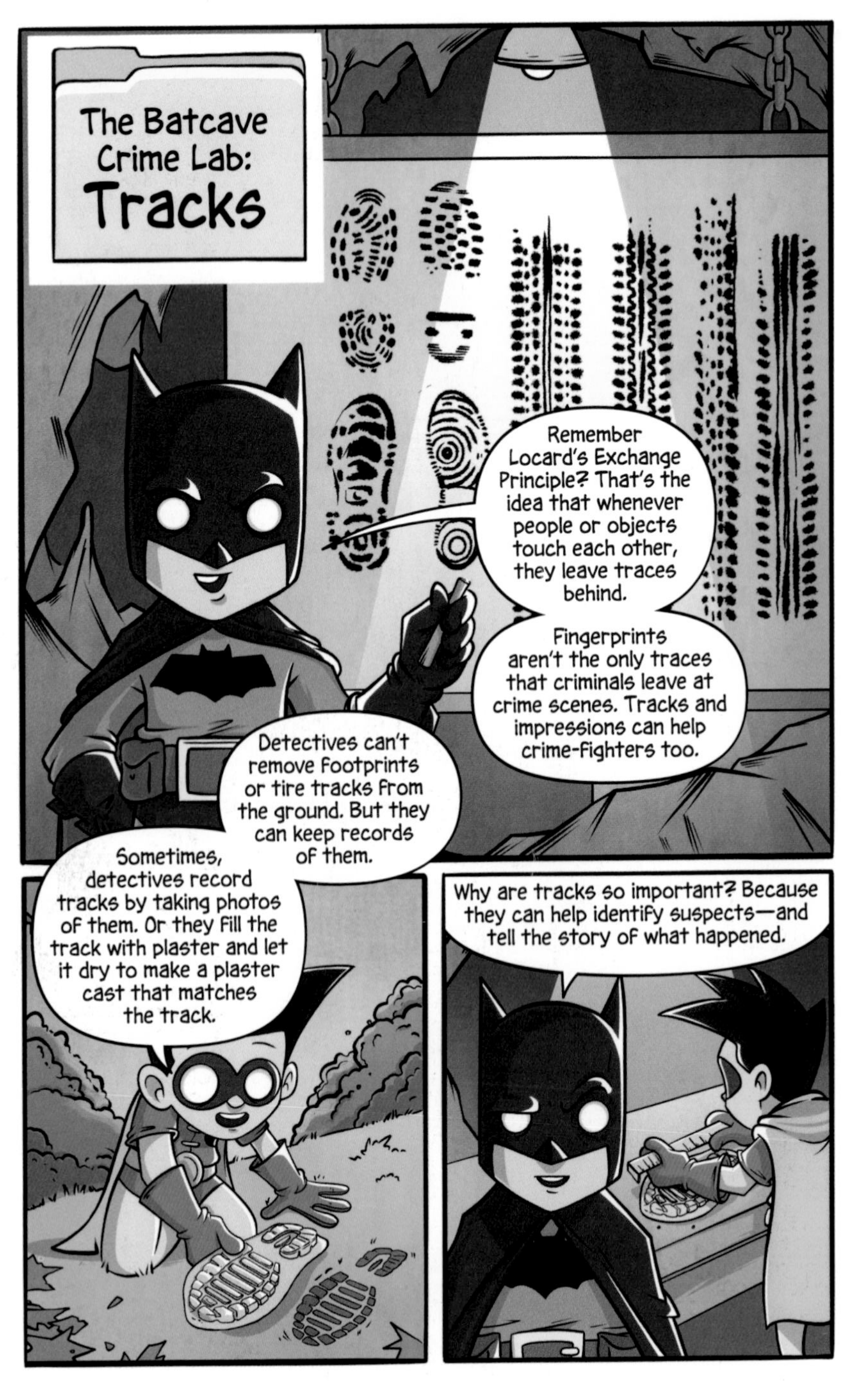
The Batcave Crime Lab: Tracks
Remember Locard's Exchange Principle? That's the idea that whenever people or objects touch each other, they leave traces behind.
Fingerprints aren't the only traces that criminals leave at crime scenes. Tracks and impressions can help crime-fighters too.
Detectives can't remove footprints or tire tracks from the ground. But they can keep records of them.
Sometimes, detectives record tracks by taking photos of them. Or they fill the track with plaster and let it dry to make a plaster cast that matches the track.
Why are tracks so important? Because they can help identify suspects—and tell the story of what happened.

Take these footprints, for example. We can try to follow them and see where the burglar went after breaking into the house. But footprints tell us much more too.
The size of the prints and the distance between them can help us estimate the criminal's height.
The depth of the prints gives us clues about how heavy the criminal might be.
When the depth changes in the middle of a row of footprints, it could mean the criminal picked up something heavy or put it down.
And when the *distance* between footprints changes, like it does here, it could mean that the criminal switched from walking to running.

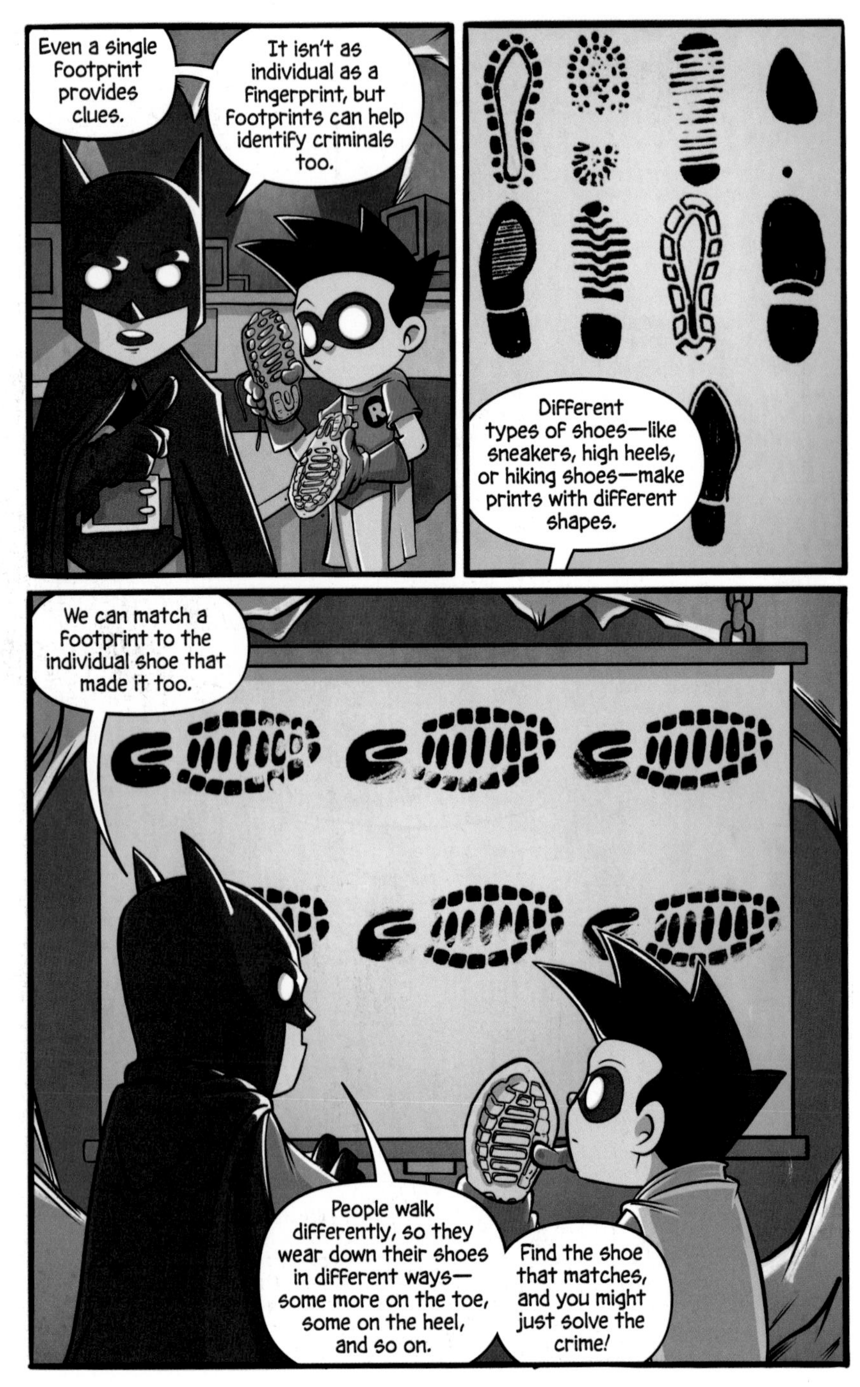
Even a single footprint provides clues.
It isn't as individual as a fingerprint, but footprints can help identify criminals too.
Different types of shoes—like sneakers, high heels, or hiking shoes—make prints with different shapes.
We can match a footprint to the individual shoe that made it too.
People walk differently, so they wear down their shoes in different ways—some more on the toe, some on the heel, and so on.
Find the shoe that matches, and you might just solve the crime!

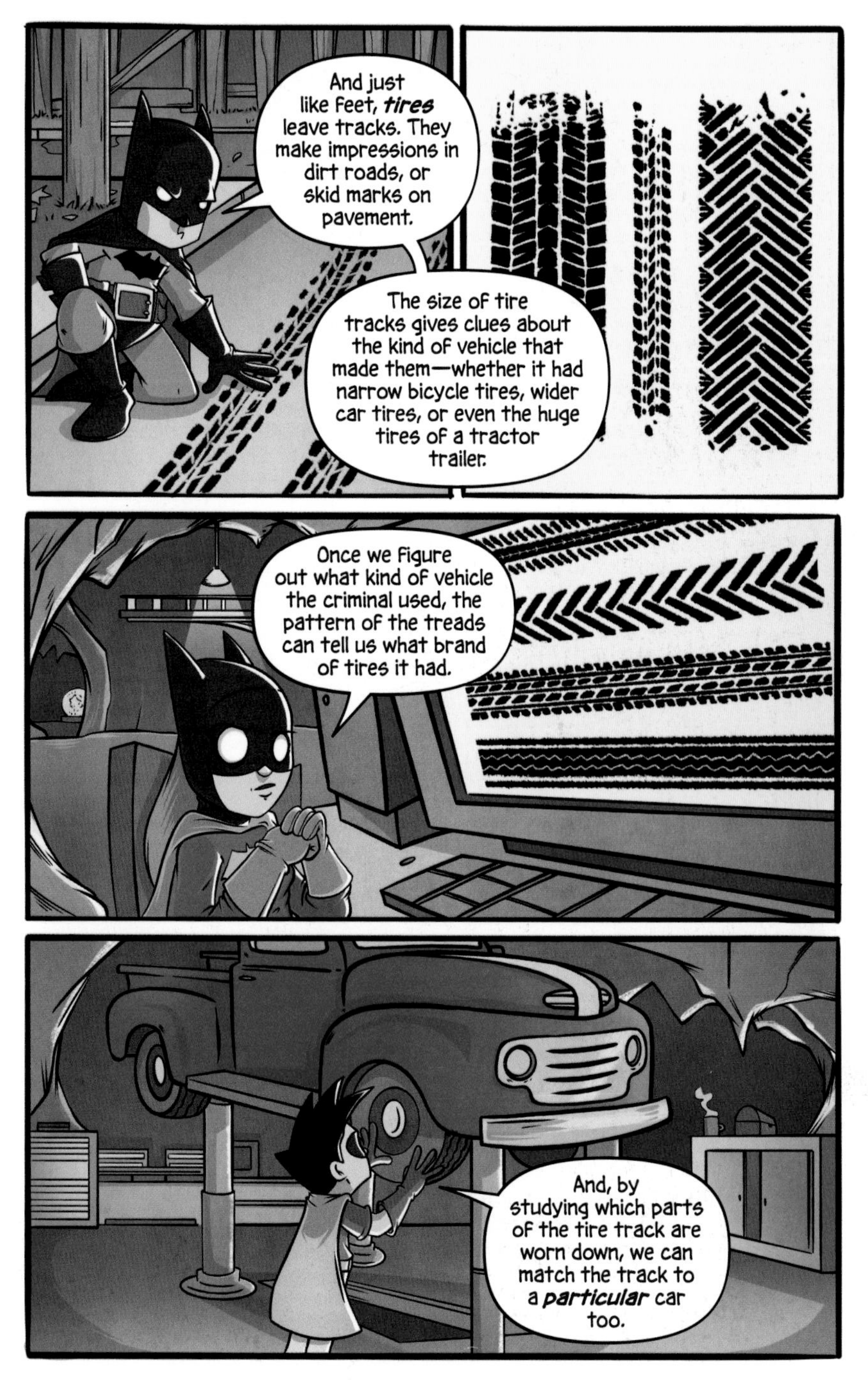
And just like feet, *tires* leave tracks. They make impressions in dirt roads, or skid marks on pavement.
The size of tire tracks gives clues about the kind of vehicle that made them—whether it had narrow bicycle tires, wider car tires, or even the huge tires of a tractor trailer.
Once we figure out what kind of vehicle the criminal used, the pattern of the treads can tell us what brand of tires it had.
And, by studying which parts of the tire track are worn down, we can match the track to a *particular* car too.

Try it yourself! Make your own footprint in mud or on a big piece of paper, and see how it compares to the bottom of your shoe.
You can even turn it into a game with your friends. Have one friend secretly make some footprints.
Then compare the prints to each other's shoes.
Can you figure out who made the footprints? You're a track detective!
Very true, Master Robin. As an amateur sleuth myself, there is only one type of footprint I find less than useful...
What's that, Alfred?
The footprints that I have to clean up from the floor of the Batcave!
Whoops, sorry.
CASE CLOSED!

Thank you, Alfred. Dinner was delicious.
My pleasure, Master Bruce. Would you care for dessert?
No time. I need to go get changed and head out on patrol.
Ah, yes. Another Friday night on the town. Complete with stylish *cape* and *cowl.*
Shall I expect you home by morning?
BINNNNGG
BONNNNNNGG
Eh? The doorbell?
Were you expecting someone?
CHAPTER 4:
The Case of the History Mystery

May I help you?
I have to see Bruce Wayne!
It's rather late. If you'd care to call tomorrow...
This can't wait until tomorrow!
Mr. Wayne has gone out. As I said, if you—
It's all right, Alfred. Let's hear what he has to say.

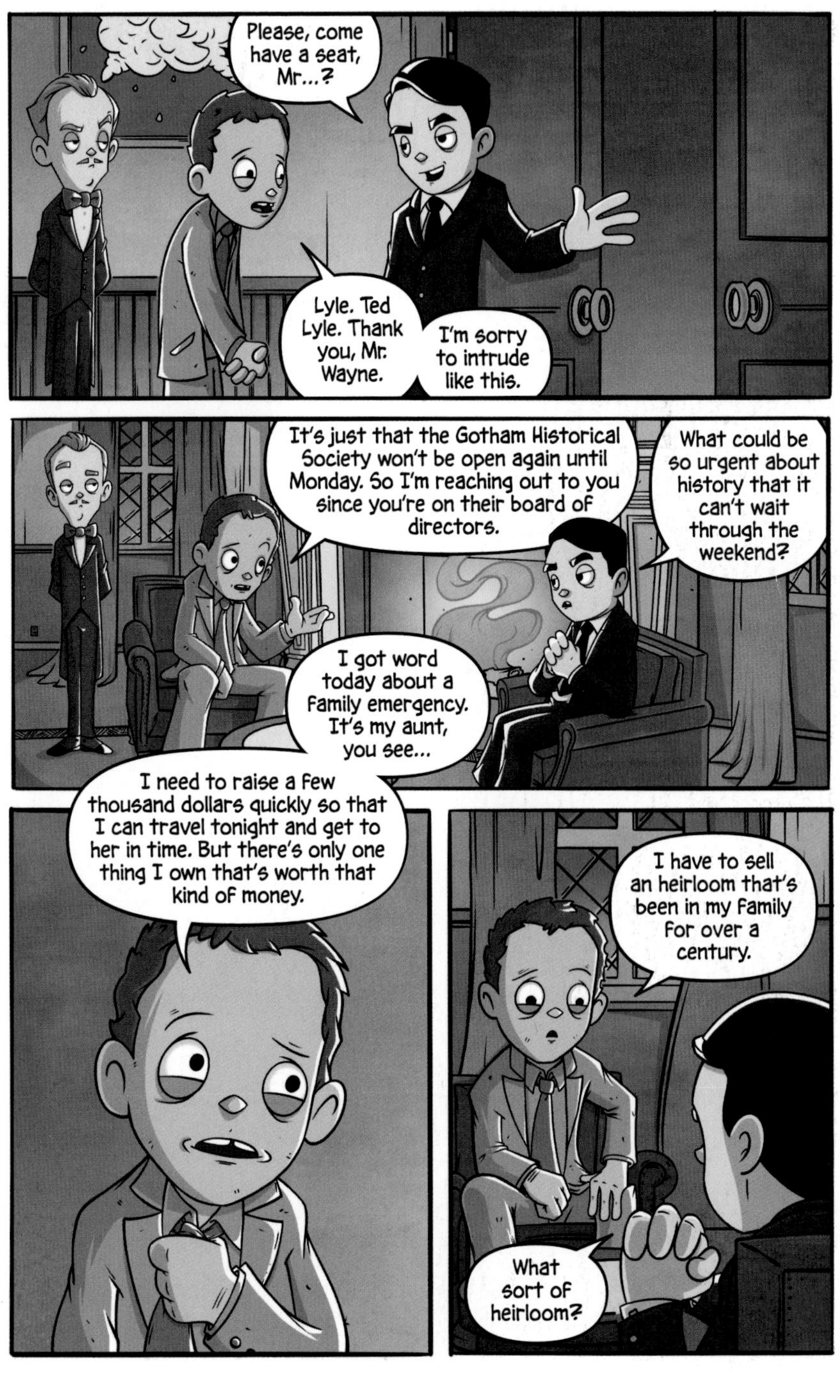
Please, come have a seat, Mr...?
Lyle. Ted Lyle. Thank you, Mr. Wayne.
I'm sorry to intrude like this.
It's just that the Gotham Historical Society won't be open again until Monday. So I'm reaching out to you since you're on their board of directors.
What could be so urgent about history that it can't wait through the weekend?
I got word today about a family emergency. It's my aunt, you see...
I need to raise a few thousand dollars quickly so that I can travel tonight and get to her in time. But there's only one thing I own that's worth that kind of money.
I have to sell an heirloom that's been in my family for over a century.
What sort of heirloom?

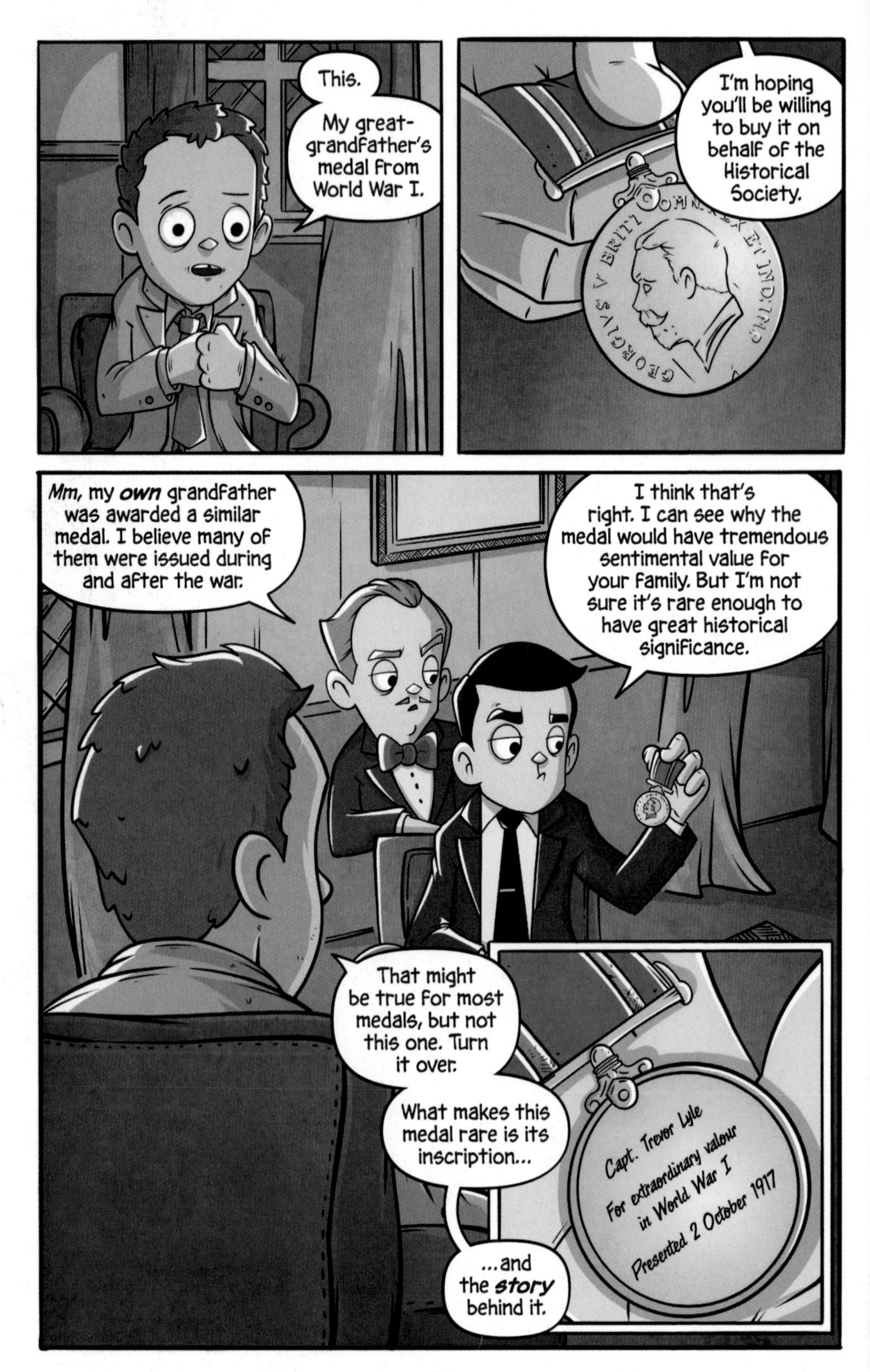
This.
My great-grandfather's medal from World War I.
I'm hoping you'll be willing to buy it on behalf of the Historical Society.
GEORGIVS V BRITT: OMN: REX ET IND: IMP:
Mm, my ***own*** grandfather was awarded a similar medal. I believe many of them were issued during and after the war.
I think that's right. I can see why the medal would have tremendous sentimental value for your family. But I'm not sure it's rare enough to have great historical significance.
That might be true for most medals, but not this one. Turn it over.
What makes this medal rare is its inscription...
...and the ***story*** behind it.
Capt. Trevor Lyle
For extraordinary valour in World War I
Presented 2 October 1917

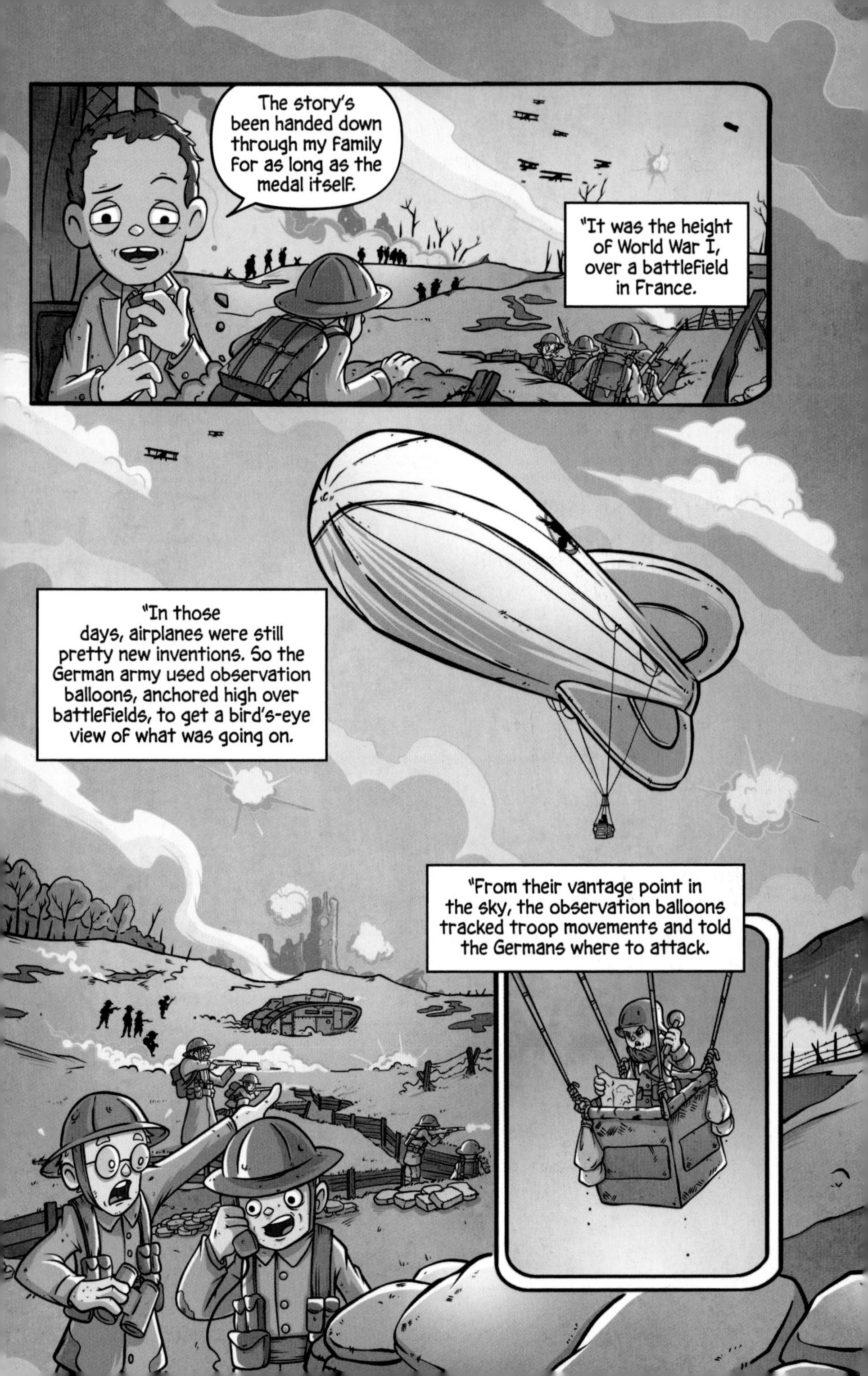
The story's been handed down through my family for as long as the medal itself.
"It was the height of World War I, over a battlefield in France.
"In those days, airplanes were still pretty new inventions. So the German army used observation balloons, anchored high over battlefields, to get a bird's-eye view of what was going on.
"From their vantage point in the sky, the observation balloons tracked troop movements and told the Germans where to attack.

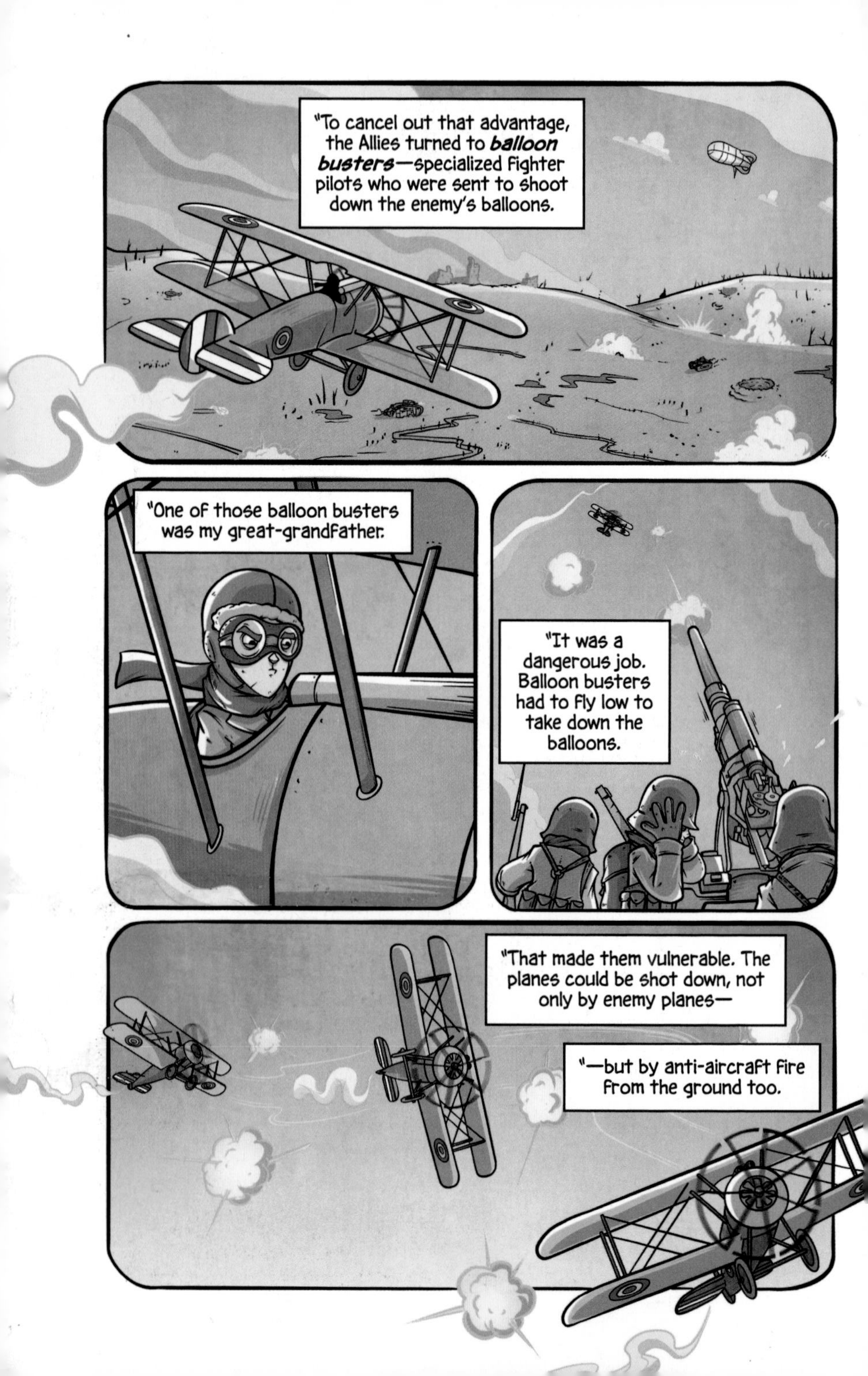
"To cancel out that advantage, the Allies turned to **balloon busters**—specialized fighter pilots who were sent to shoot down the enemy's balloons.
"One of those balloon busters was my great-grandfather.
"It was a dangerous job. Balloon busters had to fly low to take down the balloons.
"That made them vulnerable. The planes could be shot down, not only by enemy planes—
"—but by anti-aircraft fire from the ground too.

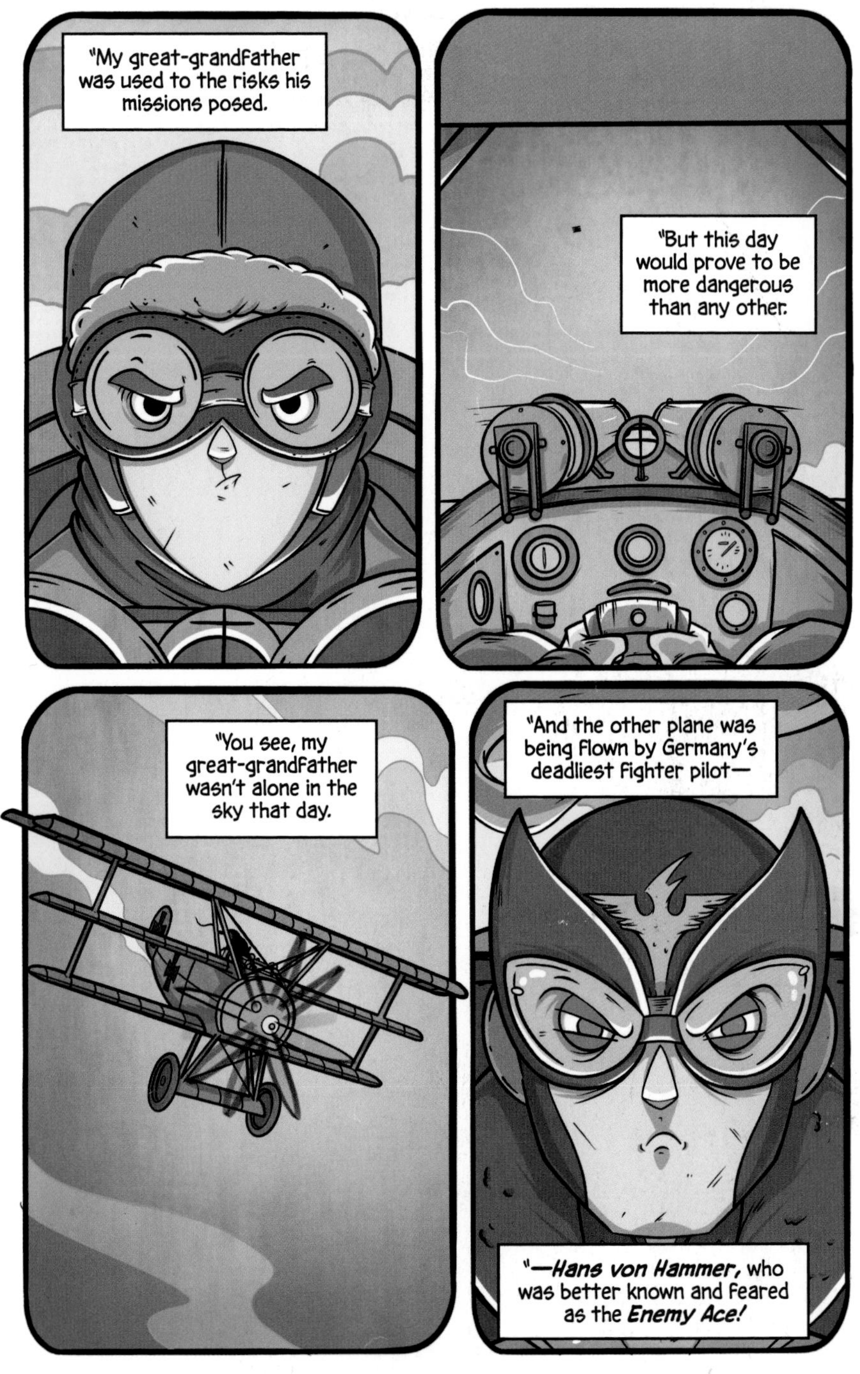
"My great-grandfather was used to the risks his missions posed.
"But this day would prove to be more dangerous than any other.
"You see, my great-grandfather wasn't alone in the sky that day.
"And the other plane was being flown by Germany's deadliest fighter pilot—
"—*Hans von Hammer*, who was better known and feared as the *Enemy Ace!*

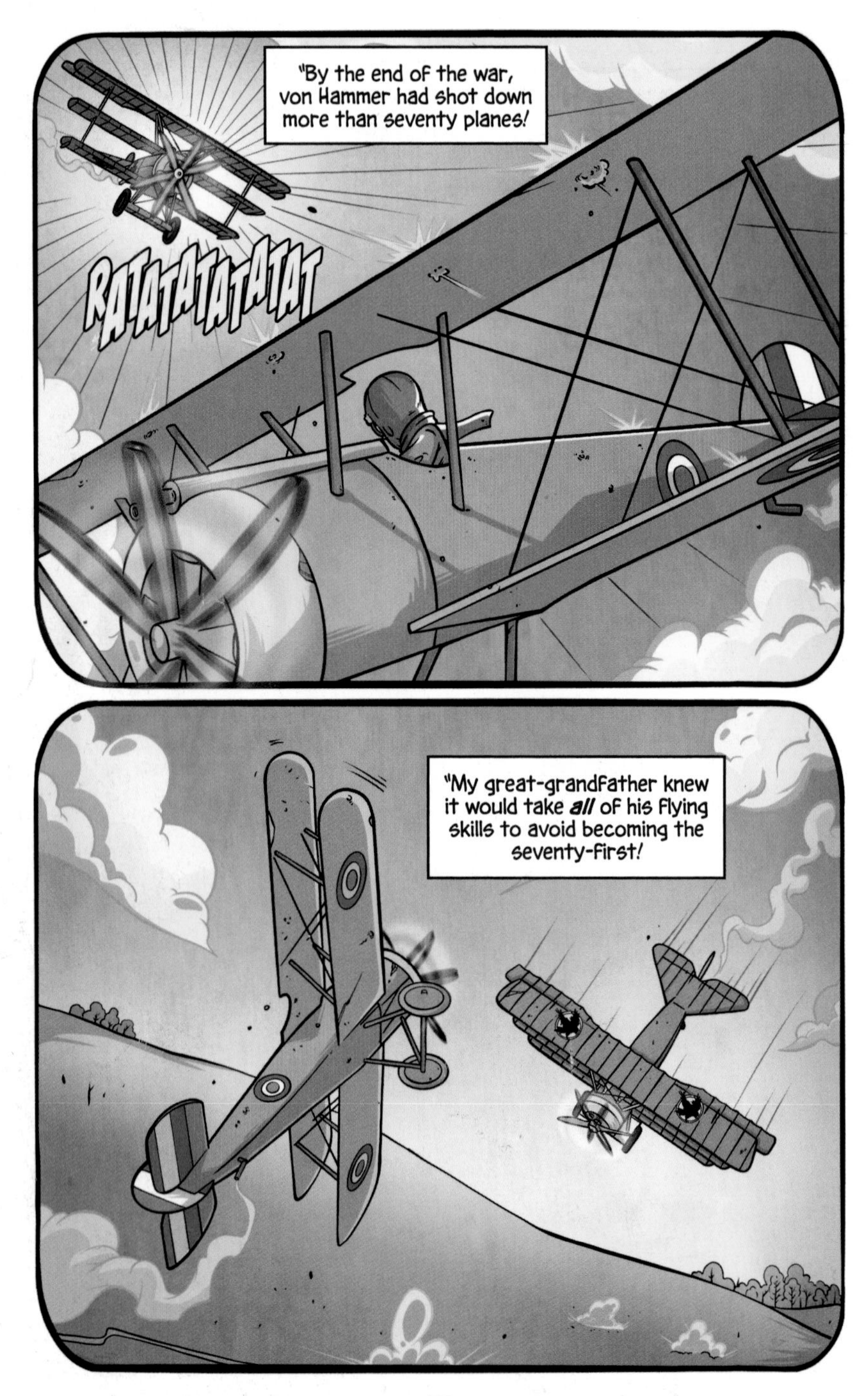
"By the end of the war, von Hammer had shot down more than seventy planes!
RATATATATATAT
"My great-grandfather knew it would take *all* of his flying skills to avoid becoming the seventy-first!

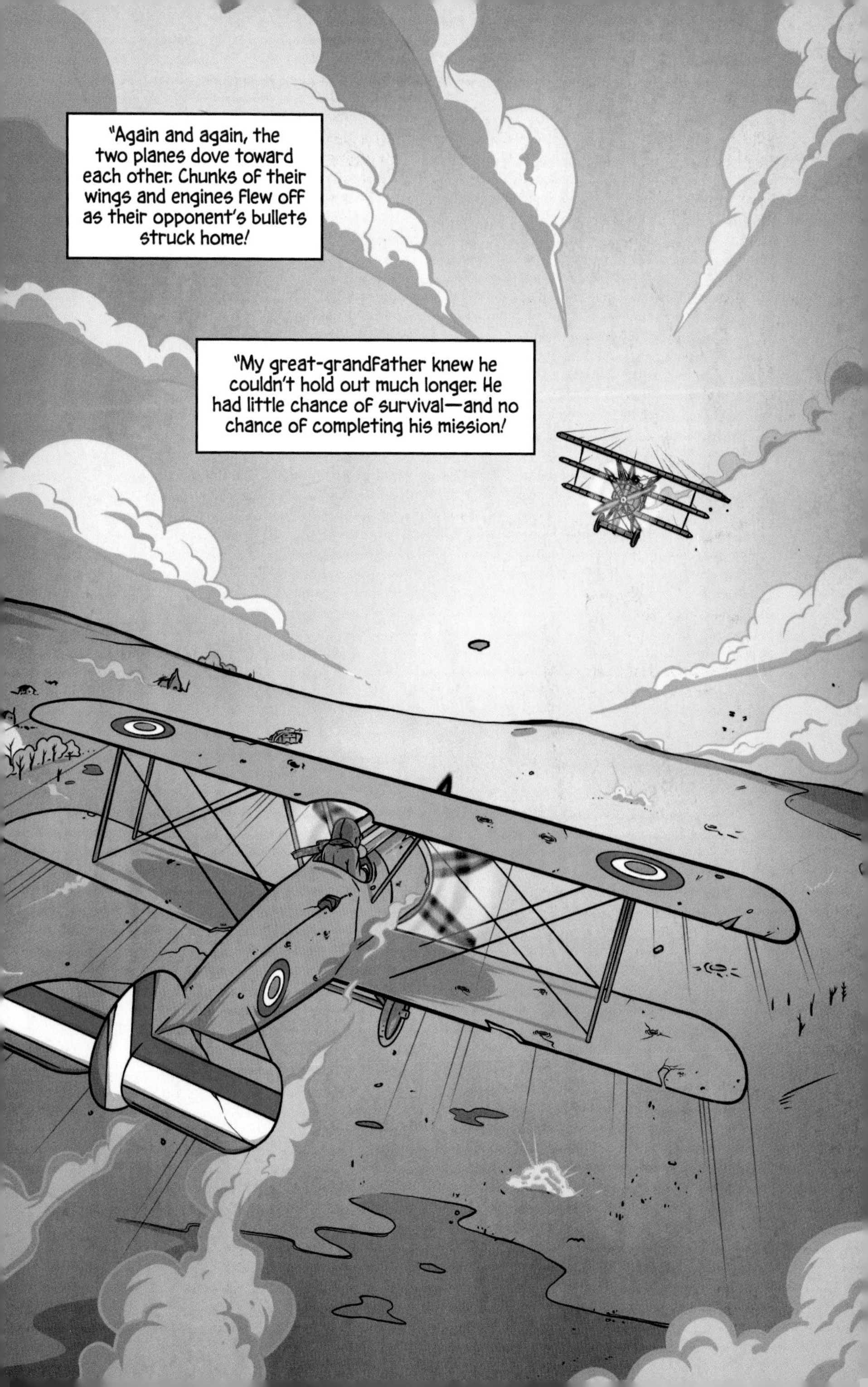

"Again and again, the two planes dove toward each other. Chunks of their wings and engines flew off as their opponent's bullets struck home!

"My great-grandfather knew he couldn't hold out much longer. He had little chance of survival—and no chance of completing his mission!

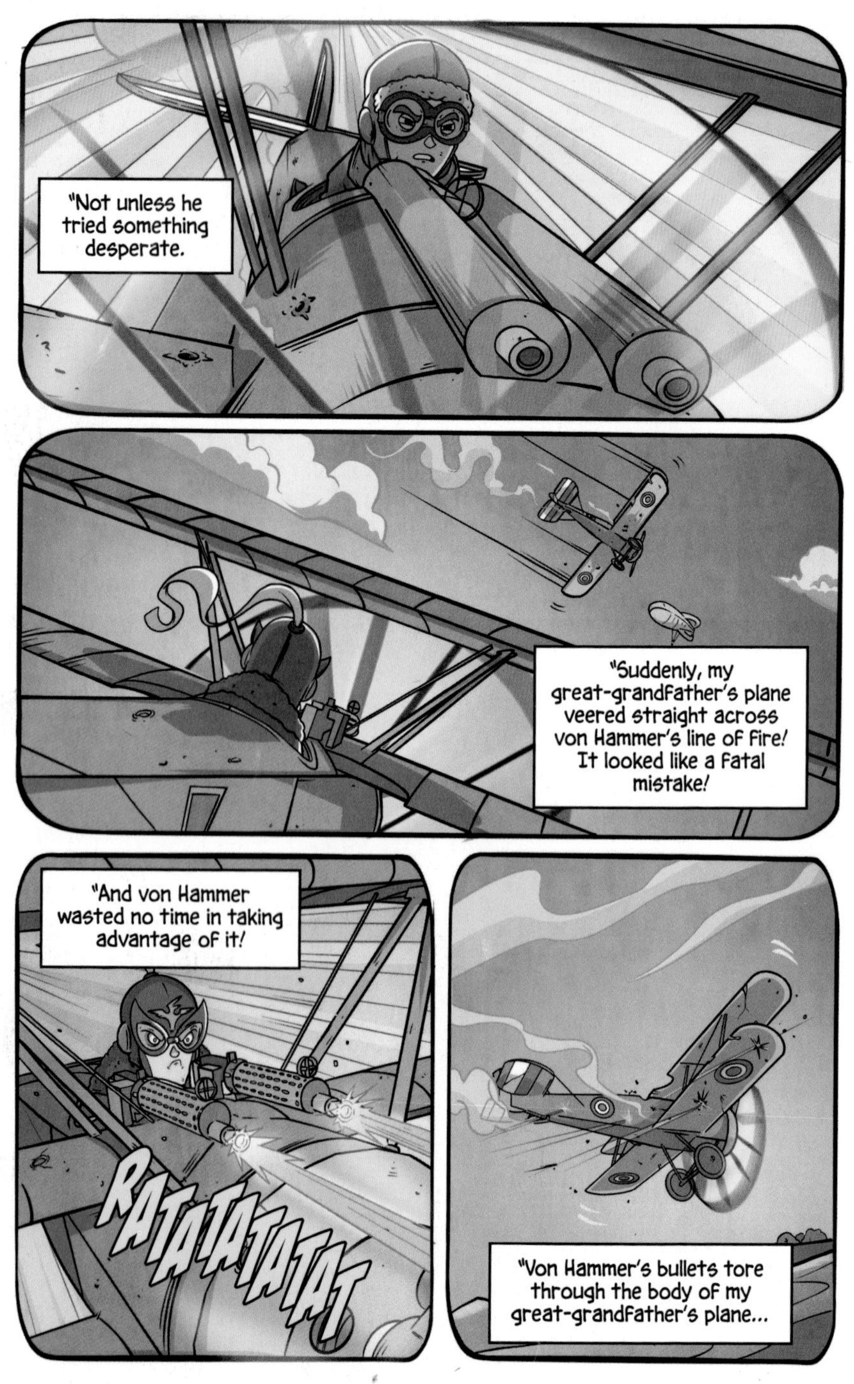
"Not unless he tried something desperate.
"Suddenly, my great-grandfather's plane veered straight across von Hammer's line of fire! It looked like a fatal mistake!
"And von Hammer wasted no time in taking advantage of it!
RATATATATATAT
"Von Hammer's bullets tore through the body of my great-grandfather's plane...

"...and straight into the German observation balloon *behind* it!
"And so, my great-grandfather's mission was accomplished. The German balloon was shot down...
BUH-
WHOOOOOMMMM
"...by its own country's greatest ace!

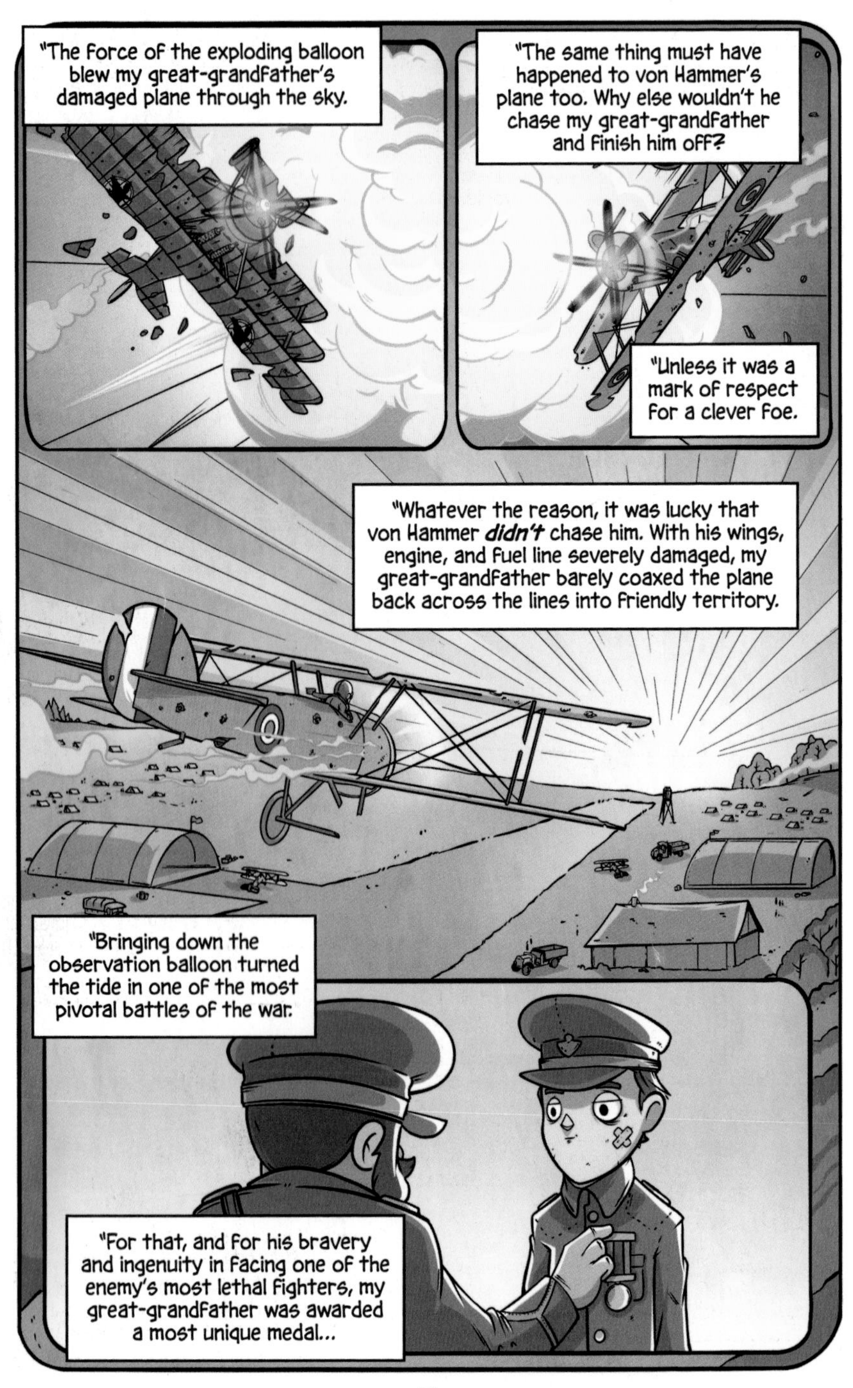
"The force of the exploding balloon blew my great-grandfather's damaged plane through the sky.
"The same thing must have happened to von Hammer's plane too. Why else wouldn't he chase my great-grandfather and finish him off?
"Unless it was a mark of respect for a clever foe.
"Whatever the reason, it was lucky that von Hammer *didn't* chase him. With his wings, engine, and fuel line severely damaged, my great-grandfather barely coaxed the plane back across the lines into friendly territory.
"Bringing down the observation balloon turned the tide in one of the most pivotal battles of the war.
"For that, and for his bravery and ingenuity in facing one of the enemy's most lethal fighters, my great-grandfather was awarded a most unique medal...

How does Bruce know the medal is a fake? Where did Ted go wrong?

Go back and review the clues. Then turn the page to check your answer.

Wh-what do you mean?
If I thought you *really* needed help for a family emergency, I would just give you the money, whether the medal was genuine or not.
But creating this forgery took time and effort. It's not something you could have put together in a couple of hours after getting an emergency call from your aunt.
That makes me doubt whether *anything* you've said is real. It's more likely that you're a con man, cheating people by selling them false antiques.
"Forgery"? "Con man"?
I don't have to stay here and listen to this!
To the contrary, I'm afraid you do.
The police responded rather swiftly when Mr. Wayne sent me to call them.

This is ridiculous! You have no proof that this medal is fake!
Actually, you handed me the proof yourself.
Your story was clever. You wove in accurate historical details to make it convincing. The Germans *did* use observation balloons during World War I, and balloon buster pilots were sent to shoot them down.
When you inscribed the medal, you even remembered to use the British spelling of "valour" and the European style of writing the date—"2 October" instead of "October 2."
But you made a mistake.
If this medal was really inscribed in 1917, it would have said "the Great War" or "the War to End All Wars," not "World War I."
The war wasn't called "World War I" until many years later.
in World War I
Presented 2 October, 1917
Indeed, Master Bruce. In 1917, no one called it "World War I" because no one knew there would ever be a World War *II*.
Bet you never thought you'd get caught by some rich guy you were trying to swindle, huh?
I guess not *every* crime has to be solved by Batman.
CASE CLOSED!

The Batcave Crime Lab: DNA
Every cell in your body contains deoxyribonucleic acid—better known as *DNA.*
DNA is much too tiny to see without a powerful microscope.
But, for something so small, DNA plays a big role in fighting crime.
DNA is like a blueprint that tells your body how tall to grow, what color eyes or hair you'll have...and just about everything physical about you.
Everyone's DNA is different. So detectives can track down suspects by matching traces of DNA that they find at a crime scene.

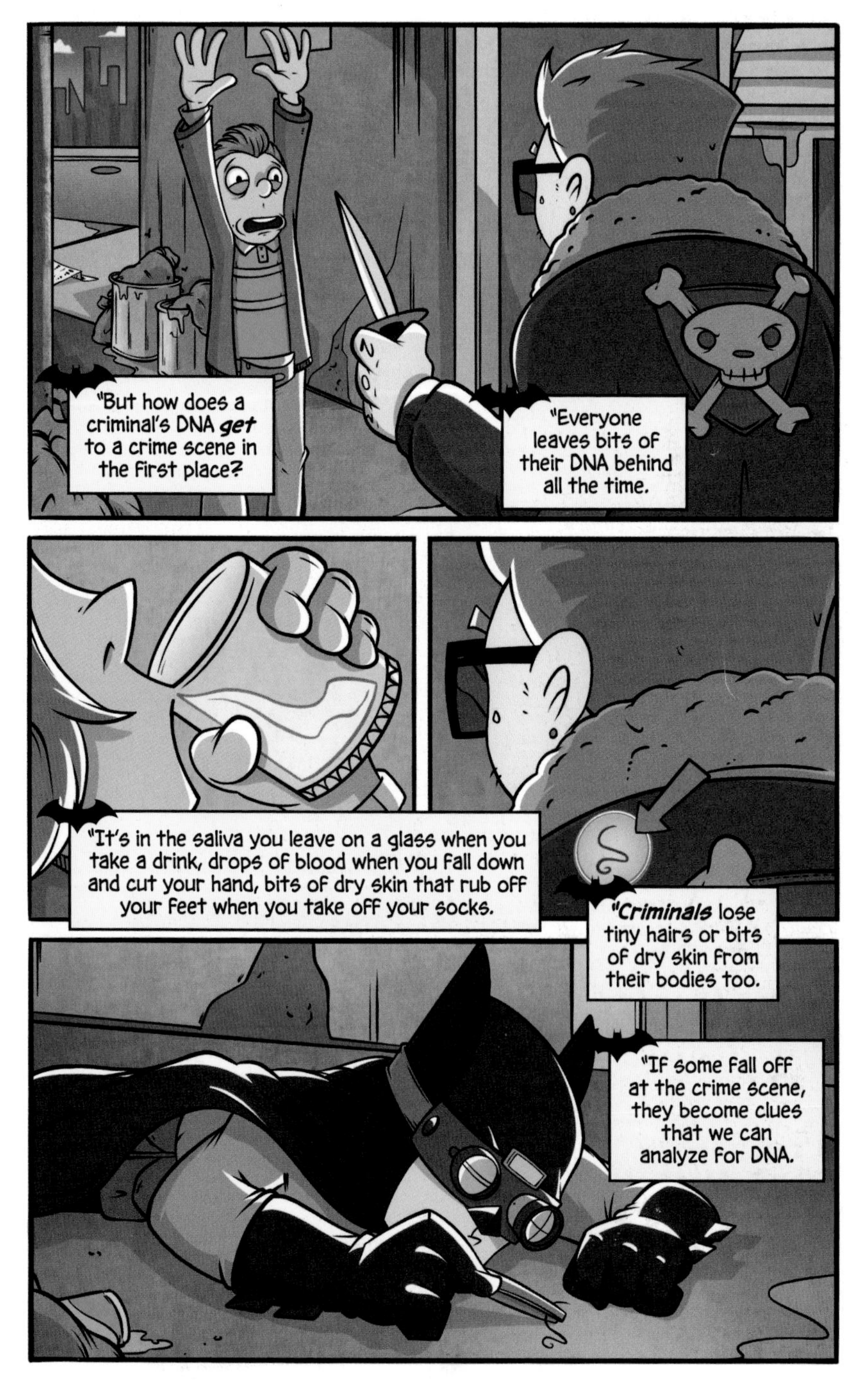
"But how does a criminal's DNA *get* to a crime scene in the first place?
"Everyone leaves bits of their DNA behind all the time.
"It's in the saliva you leave on a glass when you take a drink, drops of blood when you fall down and cut your hand, bits of dry skin that rub off your feet when you take off your socks.
"*Criminals* lose tiny hairs or bits of dry skin from their bodies too.
"If some fall off at the crime scene, they become clues that we can analyze for DNA.

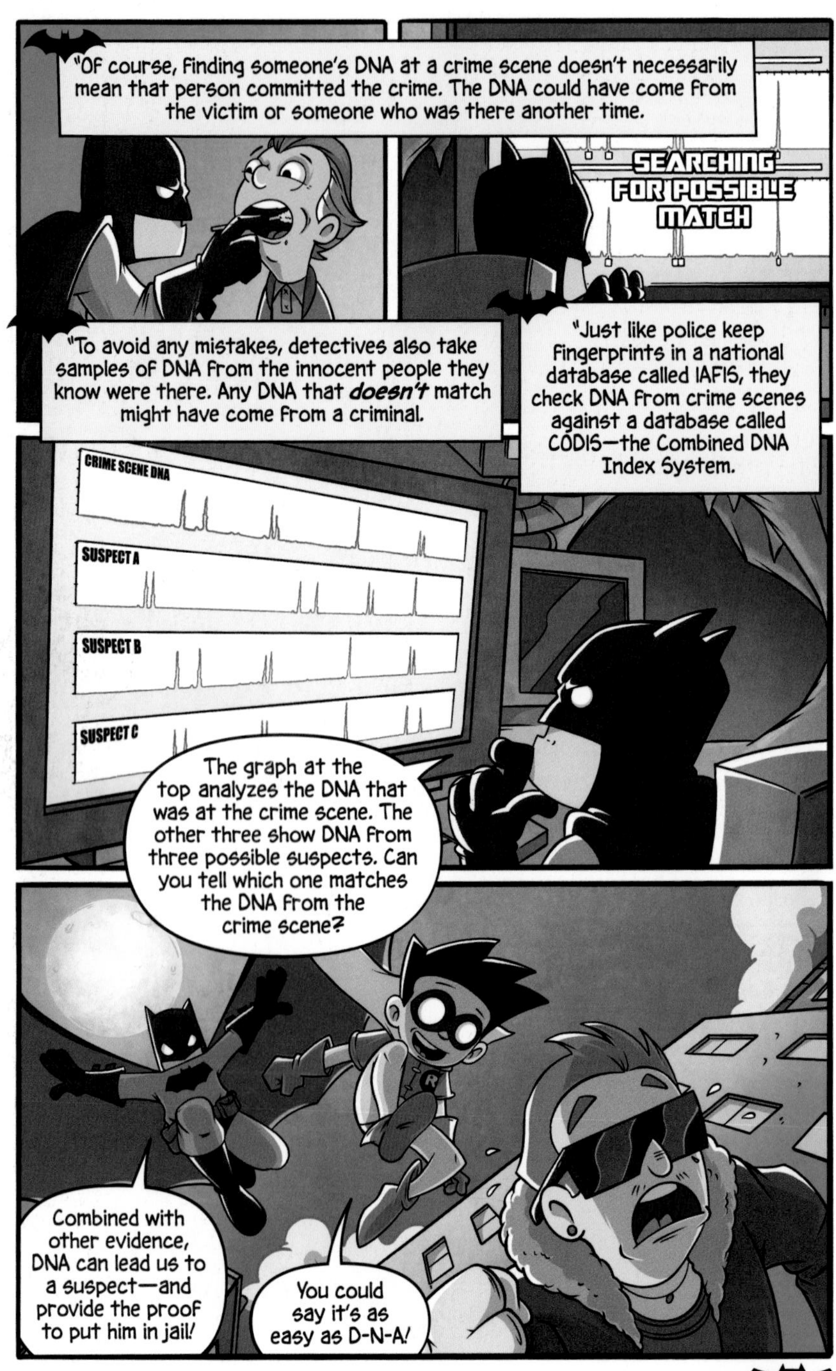
"Of course, finding someone's DNA at a crime scene doesn't necessarily mean that person committed the crime. The DNA could have come from the victim or someone who was there another time.
SEARCHING FOR POSSIBLE MATCH
"To avoid any mistakes, detectives also take samples of DNA from the innocent people they know were there. Any DNA that *doesn't* match might have come from a criminal.
"Just like police keep fingerprints in a national database called IAFIS, they check DNA from crime scenes against a database called CODIS—the Combined DNA Index System.
CRIME SCENE DNA
SUSPECT A
SUSPECT B
SUSPECT C
The graph at the top analyzes the DNA that was at the crime scene. The other three show DNA from three possible suspects. Can you tell which one matches the DNA from the crime scene?
Combined with other evidence, DNA can lead us to a suspect—and provide the proof to put him in jail!
You could say it's as easy as D-N-A!

CASE CLOSED!

A blanket of fresh snow is fine on a quiet winter's evening.
Even dangling icicles just complete the scene.
But snow and icicles mean something very different when they're *indoors.*
That's the hallmark of a bank robbery by Gotham City's most chilling villain...
FWAAAAAASSSSHHHHH

THOOM
THOOM
Mr. Freeze!
SPAKOOOMM
CHAPTER 5:
The Case of the
Cold Cash

Even solid steel turns brittle and shatters in my icy grip. Now, to gather some cold cash...
KRASSSHHH
Batman!

Compared to your usual crimes, robbing a bank seems a little...ordinary, Freeze.
My experiments in cryogenics require rare and expensive equipment. The funds from tonight's robbery are necessary to make my work possible.
But how...?
How did I get inside? The doors were locked, but the skylight gave me a way in.
How did I know you were robbing the bank? You weren't exactly subtle.
"The bank's alarm was deactivated so that it didn't go off.
But the noise of smashing through a heavy vault door was hard to miss.
Even two blocks away!

I'll keep that in mind next time.
There won't *be* a next time!
True. There won't be...
...for *you!*

That was *too* close! Good thing this sprinkler pipe was handy.
FWAAAASSSHH
Even if it's not strong enough to support my weight for more than a moment.
Nngh!
My ankle! But no time to worry about that!
Have to move before it's...

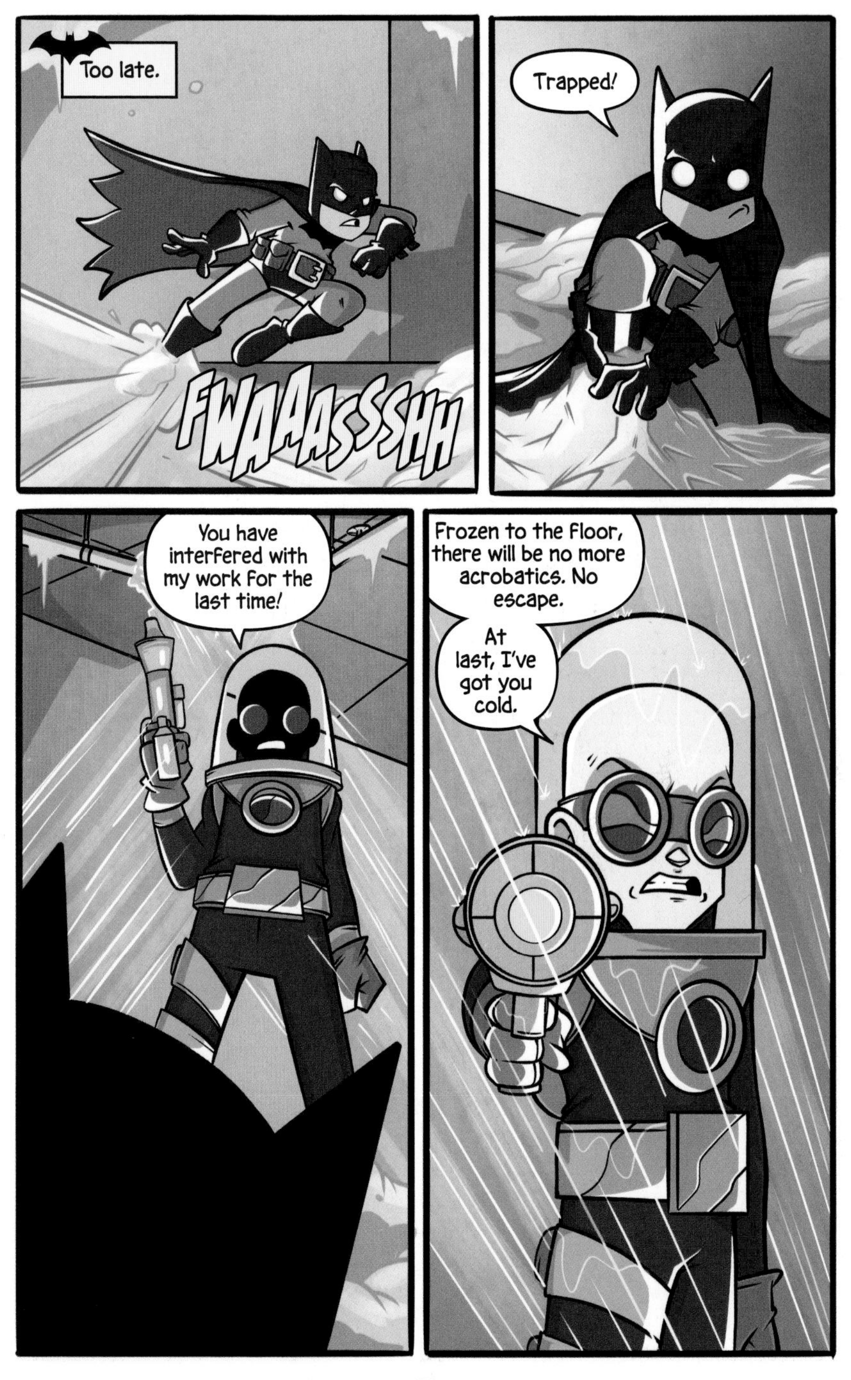
Too late.
FWAAASSSHH
Trapped!
You have interfered with my work for the last time!
Frozen to the floor, there will be no more acrobatics. No escape.
At last, I've got you cold.

I wouldn't do that.
Ever defiant, I see. I suppose this is the point when you vow vengeance.
Or when you try to keep me talking long enough to free yourself.
Forgive me if I don't give you the chance.

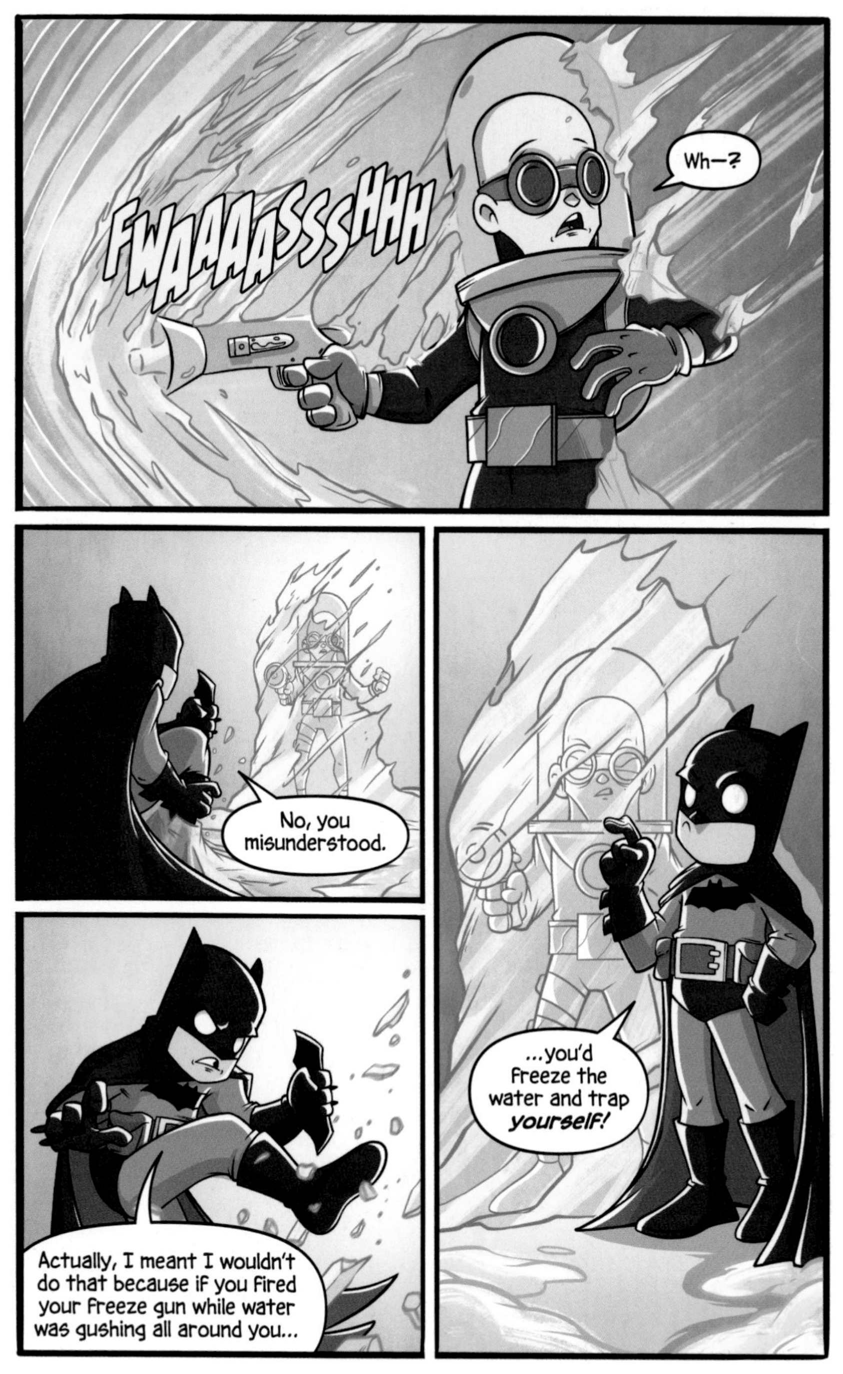
FWAAAASSSHHH
Wh—?
No, you misunderstood.
Actually, I meant I wouldn't do that because if you fired your freeze gun while water was gushing all around you...
...you'd freeze the water and trap *yourself!*

The ice will melt after a while. But it should keep you out of commission long enough for the police to take you into custody.
ACHOO!
Another one? Come out with your hands up!
No, no! I'm not a robber! I'm Martin Bessel, the bank's assistant manager!
Isn't it a little late for you to be here? The bank's been closed for hours.
Sure, but I forgot my briefcase when I left for the day. I came back to get it and found the two of you in the middle of that fight!
So, well...I hid. Luckily, neither of you noticed me until now.
Wow, there's a lot of damage. The vault door, pipes, skylight...not to mention all this snow and ice to clean up.
But I guess it'd be a lot worse if Mr. Freeze succeeded in robbing the vault too.

Thank you, Batman. I'll call the police and have them come arrest Mr. Freeze.
Don't forget to have them arrest his *accomplice* too.
"Accomplice"? Who?
You!
M-me? Th-that's ridiculous!
I don't know what Mr. Freeze told you, but he's a convicted felon! You can't take his word over mine!
It wasn't what Freeze said. It was what *you* said that supplied the clue.
STOP!
DON'T TURN THE PAGE!
?
How does Batman know?
Go back over the clues and see if *you* can solve the mystery. Then, turn the page to check if you're right.

What makes you think that Mr. Freeze even *had* an accomplice? He was clearly working alone!
I don't think so. The doors were locked when I arrived. I had to climb the outside of the building and come in through the skylight.
Not to mention that the bank's burglar alarm never went off.
"So how did Freeze get in and deactivate the alarm? The alarm box isn't frozen. He couldn't have climbed the outside of the building in his heavy armor. And he didn't shatter the outside doors like the vault.
All of the evidence suggests that Freeze had an accomplice on the inside who opened the door and turned off the alarm.
An assistant manager could do that!
Maybe, but there are other employees with access, too. Even if Mr. Freeze did have an accomplice, that doesn't mean it was me!

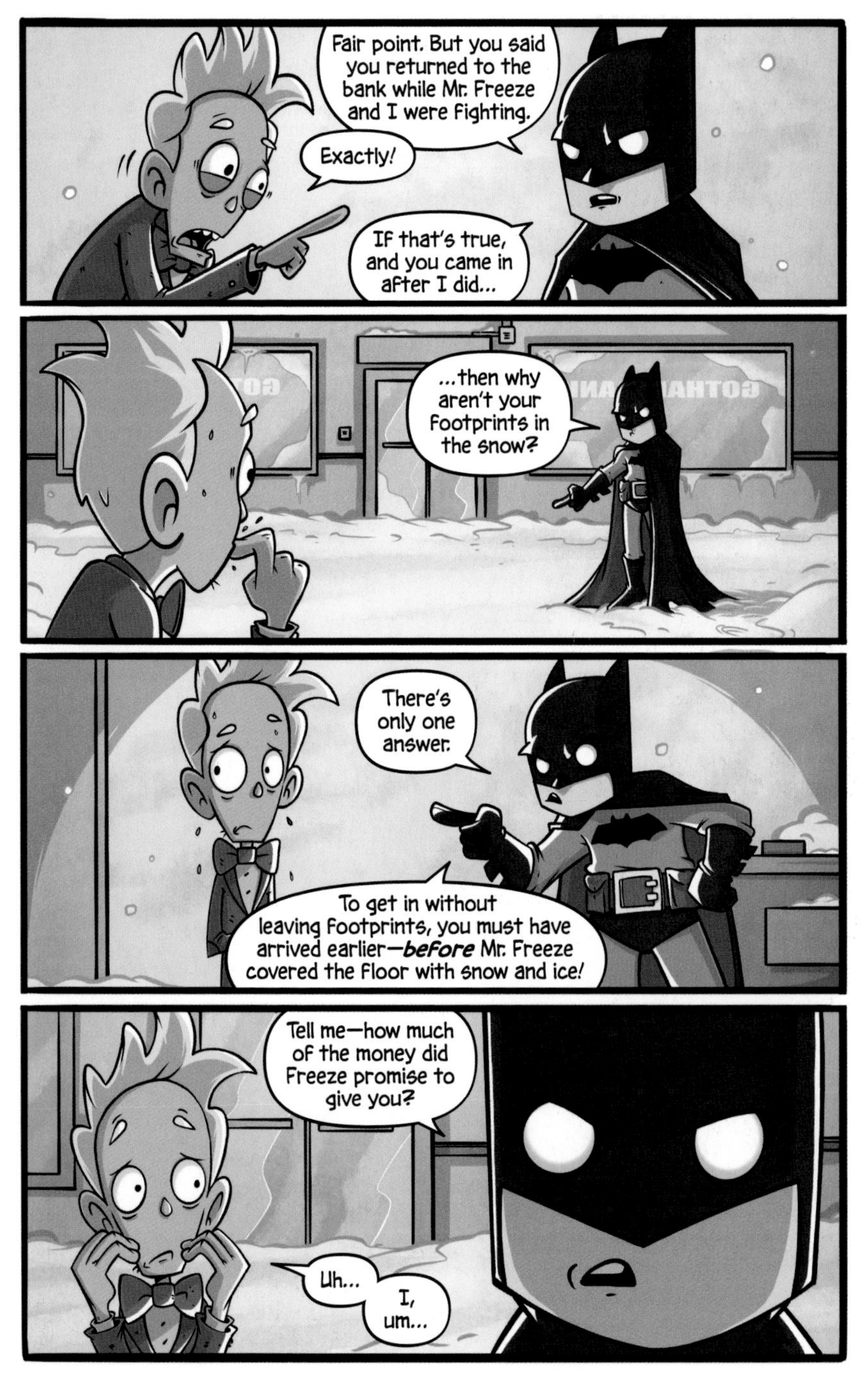
Fair point. But you said you returned to the bank while Mr. Freeze and I were fighting.
Exactly!
If that's true, and you came in after I did...
...then why aren't your footprints in the snow?
There's only one answer.
To get in without leaving footprints, you must have arrived earlier—*before* Mr. Freeze covered the floor with snow and ice!
Tell me—how much of the money did Freeze promise to give you?
Uh...
I, um...

Running away?
Really?
Got to—
Whooooooaaaaa!
Not much of a getaway. Apparently, as you began your criminal career, you failed to realize something important...
Crime is a slippery business.
CASE CLOSED!

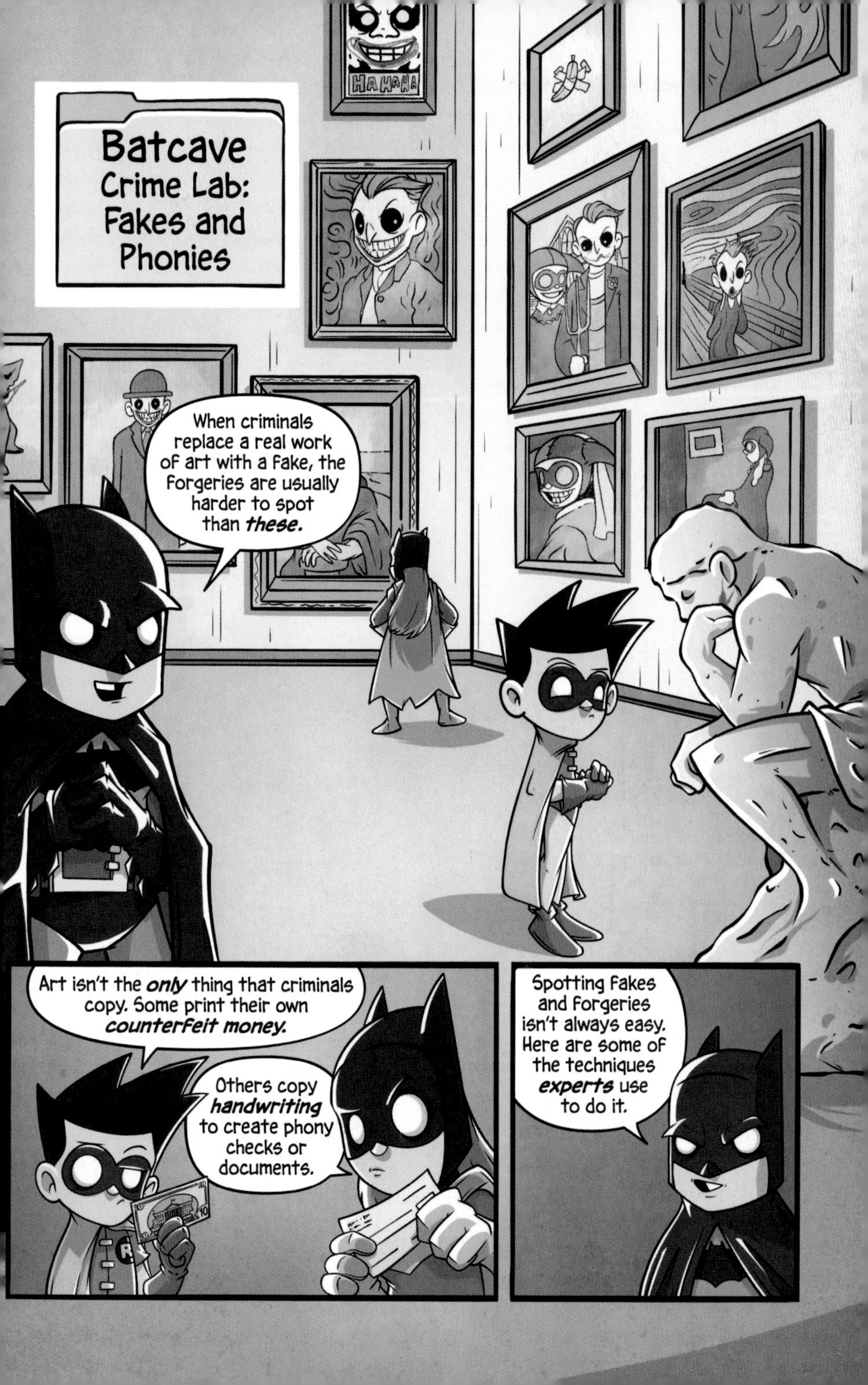
Batcave Crime Lab: Fakes and Phonies
HA HA HA
When criminals replace a real work of art with a fake, the forgeries are usually harder to spot than these.
Art isn't the only thing that criminals copy. Some print their own counterfeit money.
Others copy handwriting to create phony checks or documents.
Spotting fakes and forgeries isn't always easy. Here are some of the techniques experts use to do it.

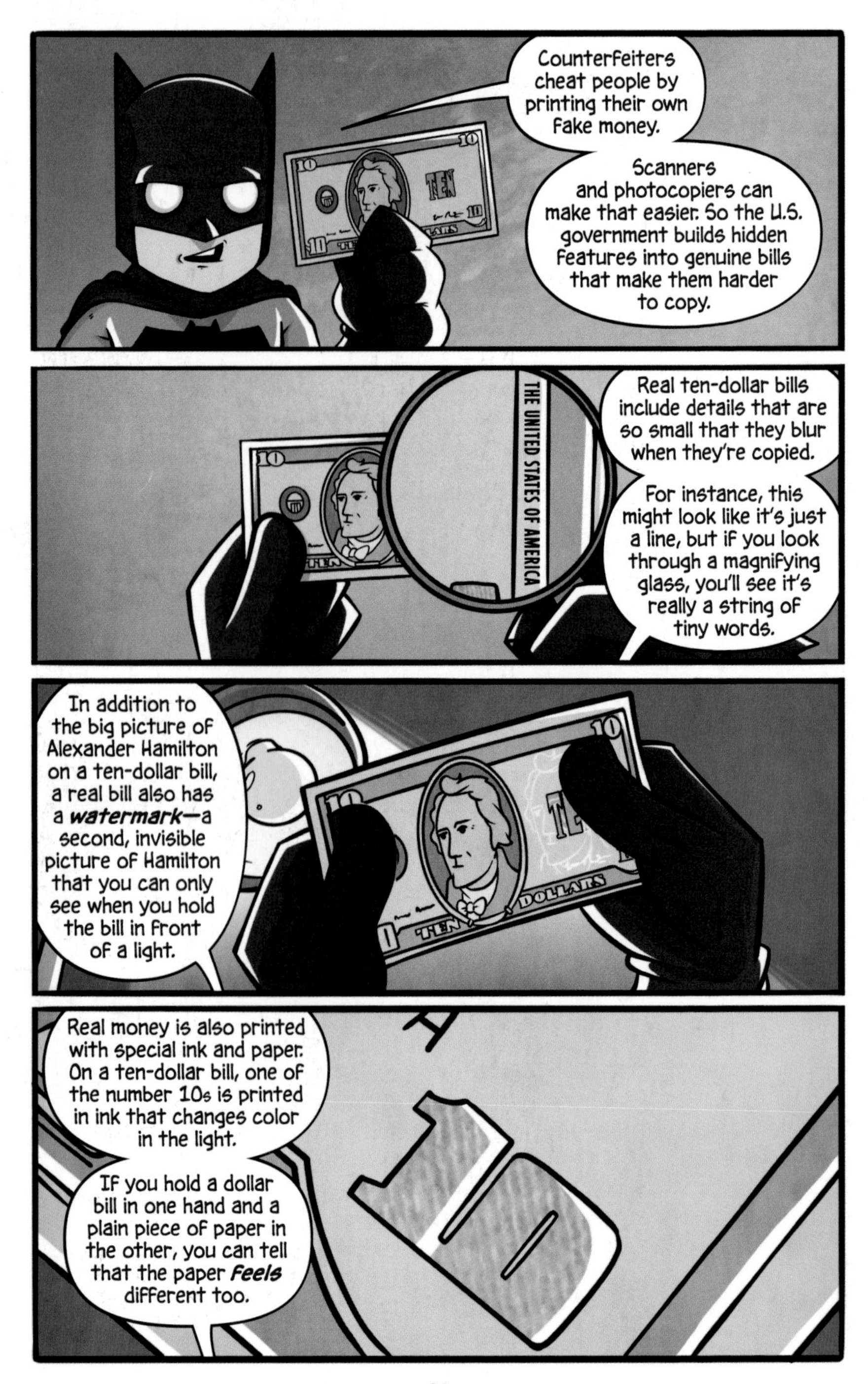
Counterfeiters cheat people by printing their own fake money.
Scanners and photocopiers can make that easier. So the U.S. government builds hidden features into genuine bills that make them harder to copy.
THE UNITED STATES OF AMERICA
Real ten-dollar bills include details that are so small that they blur when they're copied.
For instance, this might look like it's just a line, but if you look through a magnifying glass, you'll see it's really a string of tiny words.
In addition to the big picture of Alexander Hamilton on a ten-dollar bill, a real bill also has a ***watermark***—a second, invisible picture of Hamilton that you can only see when you hold the bill in front of a light.
Real money is also printed with special ink and paper. On a ten-dollar bill, one of the number 10s is printed in ink that changes color in the light.
If you hold a dollar bill in one hand and a plain piece of paper in the other, you can tell that the paper ***feels*** different too.

Some fakes are written by hand, not printed. Forgers copy people's handwriting to create phony signatures, notes, or documents.
To tell whether a signature or document is real, experts compare the handwriting to a sample—something they know was written by the actual person.
"They compare the size and shape of individual letters. They also look at how much the letters are slanted and which direction they lean.
Bruce Wayne
215
Bruce Wayne
"Besides the shapes of the individual letters, experts also check *where* the words are, like whether they're written above the lines or extend below them.
Hello Mr. Wayne,
I have recieved your letter and
we understand
"They also pay attention to the content of what's written—for example, whether the real person misspells the same words."

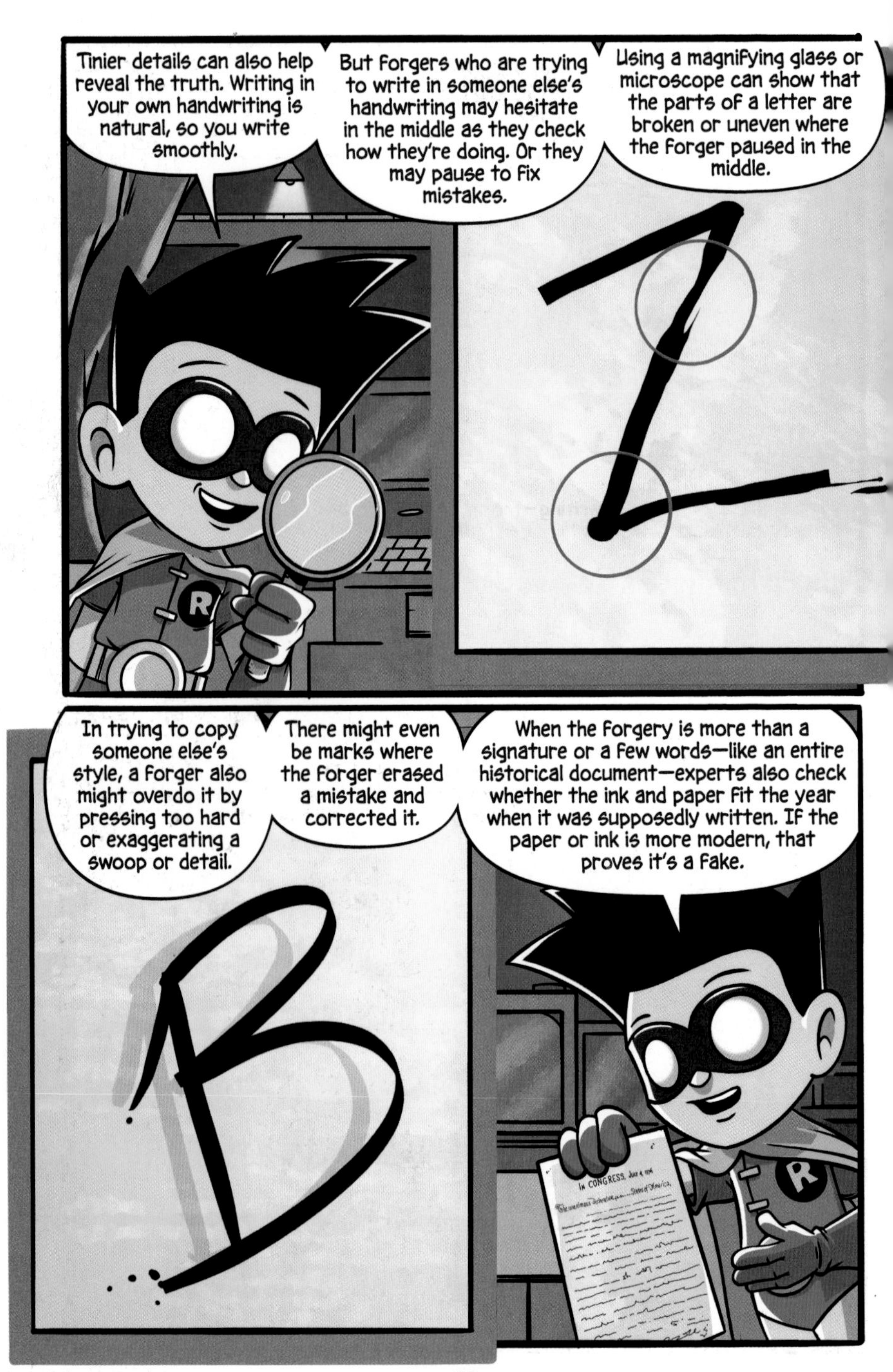
Tinier details can also help reveal the truth. Writing in your own handwriting is natural, so you write smoothly.
But forgers who are trying to write in someone else's handwriting may hesitate in the middle as they check how they're doing. Or they may pause to fix mistakes.
Using a magnifying glass or microscope can show that the parts of a letter are broken or uneven where the forger paused in the middle.
In trying to copy someone else's style, a forger also might overdo it by pressing too hard or exaggerating a swoop or detail.
There might even be marks where the forger erased a mistake and corrected it.
When the forgery is more than a signature or a few words—like an entire historical document—experts also check whether the ink and paper fit the year when it was supposedly written. If the paper or ink is more modern, that proves it's a fake.
IN CONGRESS, JULY 4, 1776

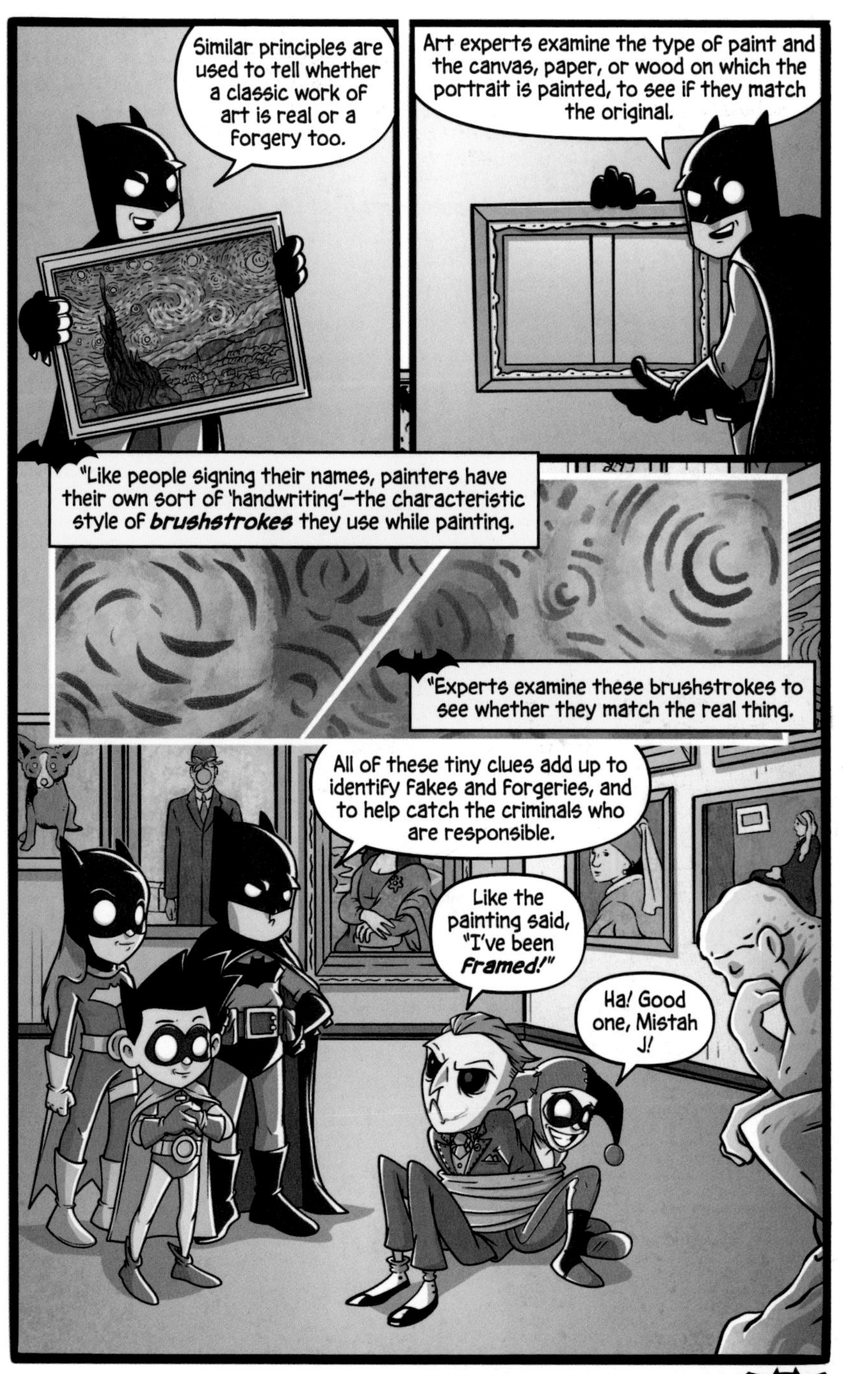
Similar principles are used to tell whether a classic work of art is real or a forgery too.
Art experts examine the type of paint and the canvas, paper, or wood on which the portrait is painted, to see if they match the original.
"Like people signing their names, painters have their own sort of 'handwriting'—the characteristic style of *brushstrokes* they use while painting.
"Experts examine these brushstrokes to see whether they match the real thing.
All of these tiny clues add up to identify fakes and forgeries, and to help catch the criminals who are responsible.
Like the painting said, "I've been *Framed!*"
Ha! Good one, Mistah J!

CASE CLOSED!

Well, *that's* done.
WAYNE TECH
Just a few hours left to finish my shift, then I'm home fr—
KELTON
Huh?
If someone's in the R&D* lab now, that could be trouble!
I'd better check it out!
*R&D = Research and Development

Hold it right there!
RESEARCH AND DEVELOPMENT NO ENTRY
B—
Batman?
Batgirl, actually.
And Robin.
Chapter 6:
The Case of the Digital Ghost

What are you two doing here? Is a super-villain robbing us?
Actually, it looks like somebody *already* robbed your R&D lab.
Judging from this broken case and the empty space on this shelf, I'd guess that some sort of prototype was taken.
What? But...but...
If the theft hasn't been reported yet, it must have happened tonight. Have you seen any intruders?
Not counting Batgirl and me, that is.
Th-that's not possible! This is a high-security area!
No alarms went off. No one can even get inside this lab without a key card!
Not counting Batgirl and me, that is.
If no alarms went off, how did *you* know to come here?
Because Batman installed his own alarms in all of WayneTech's high-tech labs. But I can't say that.
That's not important right now. The important thing is finding out who took the prototype and then getting it back.

⸗Gulp⸗ You're right!
If we don't get it back before the bosses arrive in the morning, I could lose my job!
Why you? You're not the *only* guard in the WayneTech building.
No, but the R&D lab is where WayneTech's newest and most secret technology is invented.
And I'm the night guard responsible for keeping it safe.
Has anyone else been on this floor tonight, uh...?
Kelton. My name is Kelton.
The offices are closed for the night. The only other person working late tonight is one of the company's engineers...
Dr. Driver!
What's all the noise in here? I'm trying to work next door!
Hey! This is a restricted area! You shouldn't be here!

We *should* be if you want us to solve this robbery!
R-robbery?
It can't be! What was stolen?
If you work here, maybe you can tell *us.* Do you know what used to be on that shelf?
Oh no...
It was the new nanochip WayneTech's been developing. It's going to revolutionize the computer industry...or it *was* going to, until now.
We'll do what we can to help you get it back. Did you see or hear anything unusual tonight?
Not until you two showed up.
I've been working late in the lab next door. I haven't left the room once tonight.
But *you're* supposed to be on guard against thieves, Kelton! Where were you? Taking a nap?
It's not *my* fault! Except for patrolling the floor during my usual eight o'clock rounds, I've been watching live video feeds from the security cameras all night!
Hmm...are there recordings from those cameras?
Of course. On the computer in the security office.
Then that sounds like our next stop!

Shortly...
Well, the computer log didn't show anyone unlocking the R&D lab with a key card. But someone could have deleted the record later.
The security video from the R&D lab isn't much use either. With the lights in the lab turned off, it was too dark to see much.
08:16 PM
Too bad the thief didn't steal anything from the lab next door. Those lights were on.
Yes, I told you—I was working in that room all night.
08:16 PM
Even fast-forwarding through the video from the hallway outside the lab doesn't really show anything.
I was hoping we'd see the thief breaking in. But the video doesn't show anyone in the hallway, all night long.
Is that the only entrance to the R&D lab?
Uh-huh. That lab doesn't even have a window.
Weird. How could the thief get in? It seems impossible.
Unless the thief faked the security video. Let's check the hallway for ourselves.

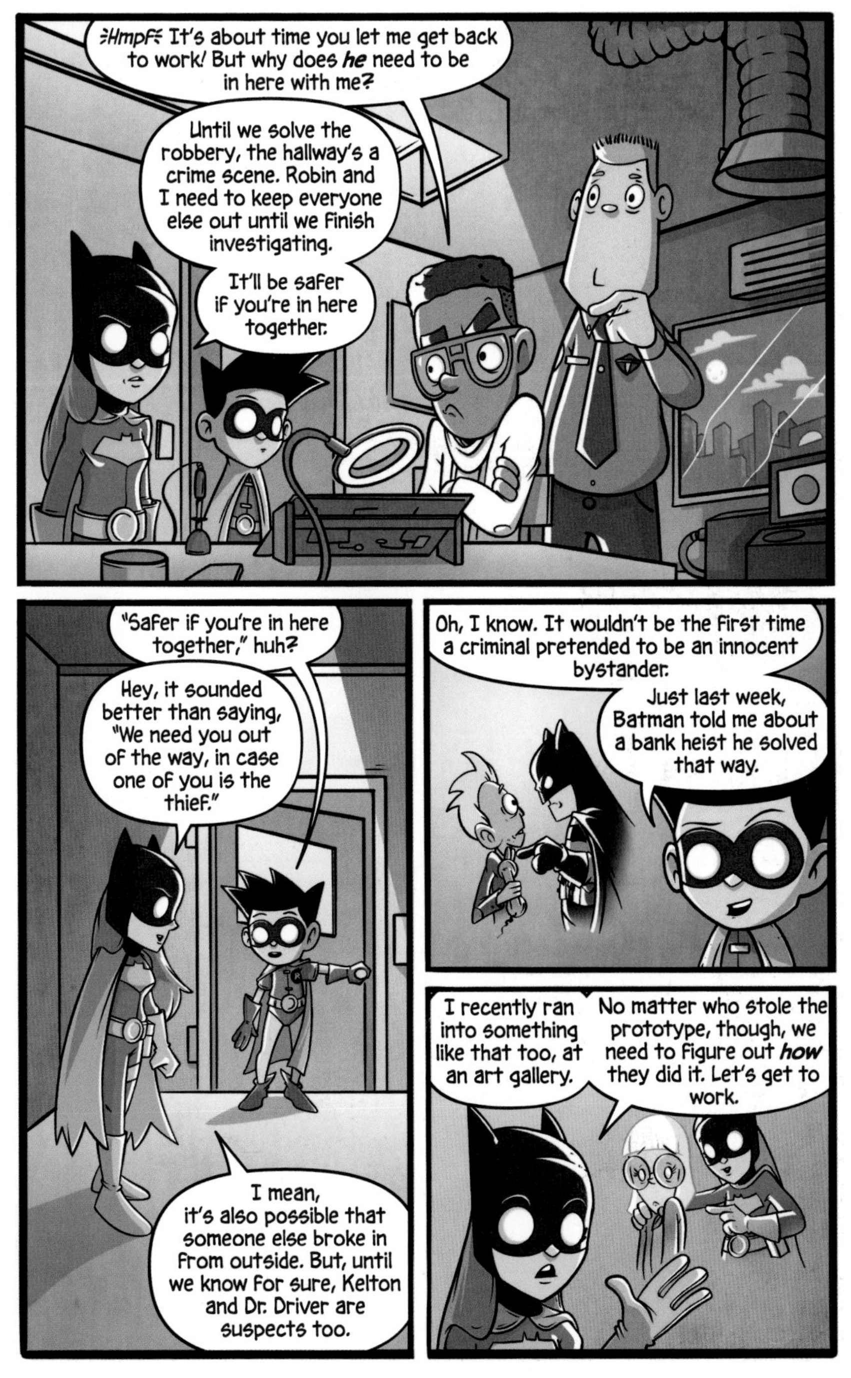
Hmpf It's about time you let me get back to work! But why does ***he*** need to be in here with me?
Until we solve the robbery, the hallway's a crime scene. Robin and I need to keep everyone else out until we finish investigating.
It'll be safer if you're in here together.
"Safer if you're in here together," huh?
Hey, it sounded better than saying, "We need you out of the way, in case one of you is the thief."
I mean, it's also possible that someone else broke in from outside. But, until we know for sure, Kelton and Dr. Driver are suspects too.
Oh, I know. It wouldn't be the first time a criminal pretended to be an innocent bystander.
Just last week, Batman told me about a bank heist he solved that way.
I recently ran into something like that too, at an art gallery.
No matter who stole the prototype, though, we need to figure out ***how*** they did it. Let's get to work.

Soon...
Nope. There are no signs that anyone tampered with this security camera.
Nothing unusual about the lab's electronic lock either. It doesn't look like anyone **broke in.**
Except for you and me, that is.
If there was no forced entry, it could mean the thief had a key.
Kelton and Dr. Driver both have key cards to unlock the lab. Maybe one of them *is* the thief.
Unless someone from outside *stole* a key card and used it to get in.
It's a mystery, all right. I have a couple of suspicions, but...
Me too, but it doesn't all quite add up yet.
Maybe we can change that.
R
R

Who do *you* think stole the prototype? And *how?*

Take another look and try to find the clues. When you think you know the answer, turn the page to check if you're right.

There! This is video of the hallway, shortly after eight o'clock tonight. Do you see the clue?
08:07 PM
What clue? There's no one in the video.
Exactly! That's the clue!
Kelton said he patrolled the floor at eight o'clock. Even if we didn't see anyone else, he should be in the video.
Say, that's right...
So, assuming you told the truth, there's only one explanation. Someone replaced that part of the video with footage from a different time...probably so no one would see them breaking into the lab!
But, as far as Batgirl and I could tell, nobody tampered with the camera in the hallway. That probably means the video footage was replaced in the security office's computer itself!

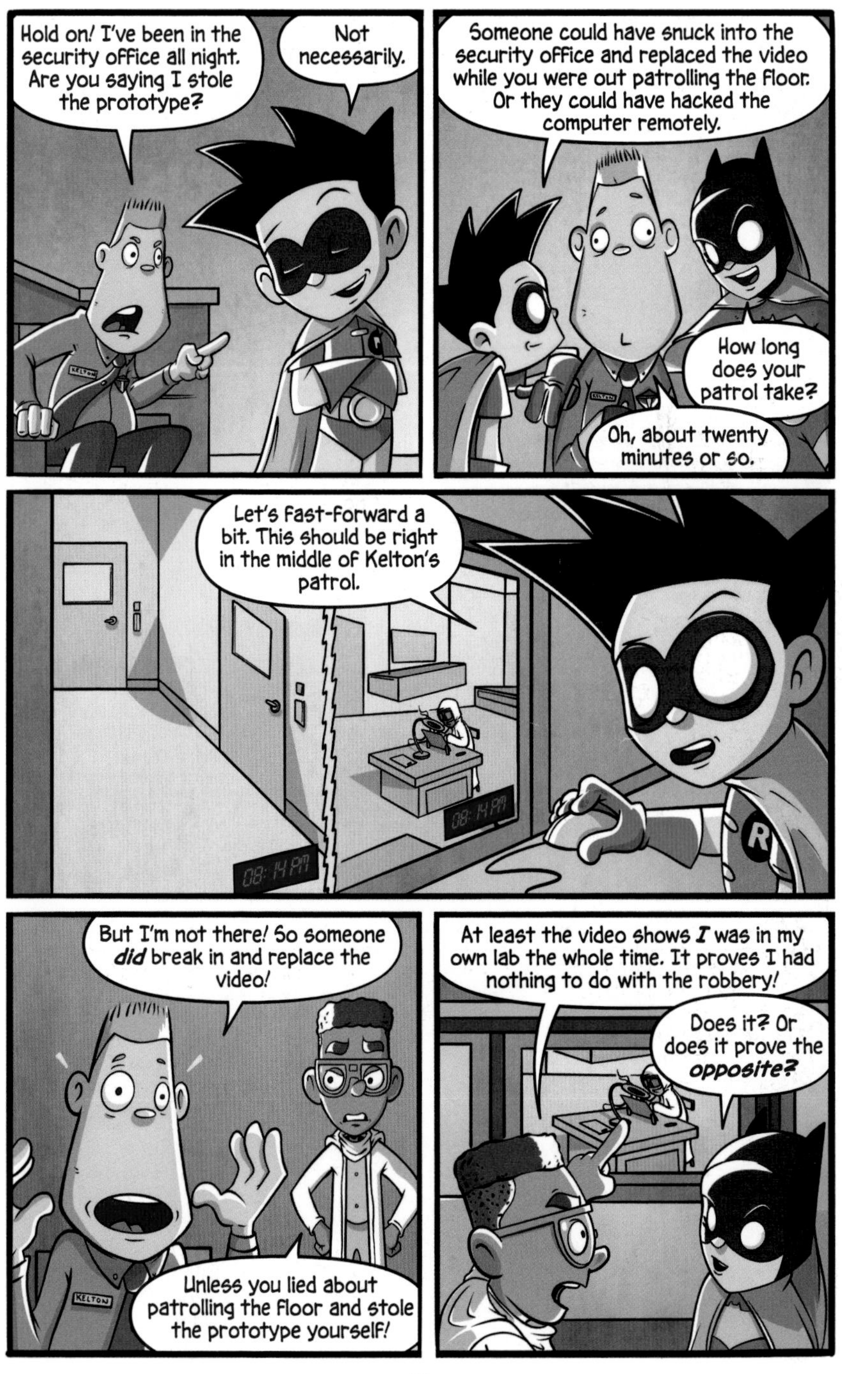
Hold on! I've been in the security office all night. Are you saying I stole the prototype?
Not necessarily.
Someone could have snuck into the security office and replaced the video while you were out patrolling the floor. Or they could have hacked the computer remotely.
How long does your patrol take?
Oh, about twenty minutes or so.
Let's fast-forward a bit. This should be right in the middle of Kelton's patrol.
08:14PM
08:14PM
But I'm not there! So someone *did* break in and replace the video!
Unless you lied about patrolling the floor and stole the prototype yourself!
At least the video shows *I* was in my own lab the whole time. It proves I had nothing to do with the robbery!
Does it? Or does it prove the ***opposite?***

What do you mean?
You'll see. Let's rewind the video a half hour or so.
This is half an hour earlier, at 7:42. Notice the shadows—they fall to the *left,* away from the overhead light.
07:42 PM
But later, the video shows the shadows falling to the *right.* Those shadows would have to come from sunlight coming through the window—which only happen in the daytime, not at night.
That means the video footage from your lab was replaced too!
08:14 PM
If Kelton stole the chip, he wouldn't need to replace *your* video. Neither would a thief from outside.
The only person who'd cover up the theft by replacing your video is *you!*
You haven't had the chance to get the chip out of the building yet. If we search, I'll bet we'll find the chip in either your lab or your pockets.
Either way, it'll be the final proof we need.
And that'll be the end of this whole *"shady"* business!
CASE CLOSED!

Batcave Crime Lab: Eyewitness Testimony
He's the one who did it!
One of the types of evidence that detectives rely on most is eyewitness testimony. Without information from people who saw the crime, it would be much harder to identify criminals and figure out what happened.
But detectives have to be careful with eyewitness testimony, because it's not always reliable. Sometimes, criminals might pretend to be witnesses themselves, and lie to cover up the crime.
And even when witnesses aren't *trying* to lie, people don't always remember everything accurately.
How good a witness are *you?* Turn the page to find out.

Take a look at this crime in progress. Study the scene for ***one minute.*** When you're done, turn the page to test your memory.
A-Z TOYS
COOKIE TIME

PAZ'S
SHAW COMICS
DIAMONDS & JEWELRY

All set? Now, use your memory to answer these questions ***without*** turning back to the previous page to check.

How many henchmen were helping the Penguin?

Which hero used a batarang?

What stores were in the mall?

What kind of birds did the Penguin use?

What color shirt did the woman in the sunglasses wear?

Which store did the Penguin's gang rob? What did they steal?

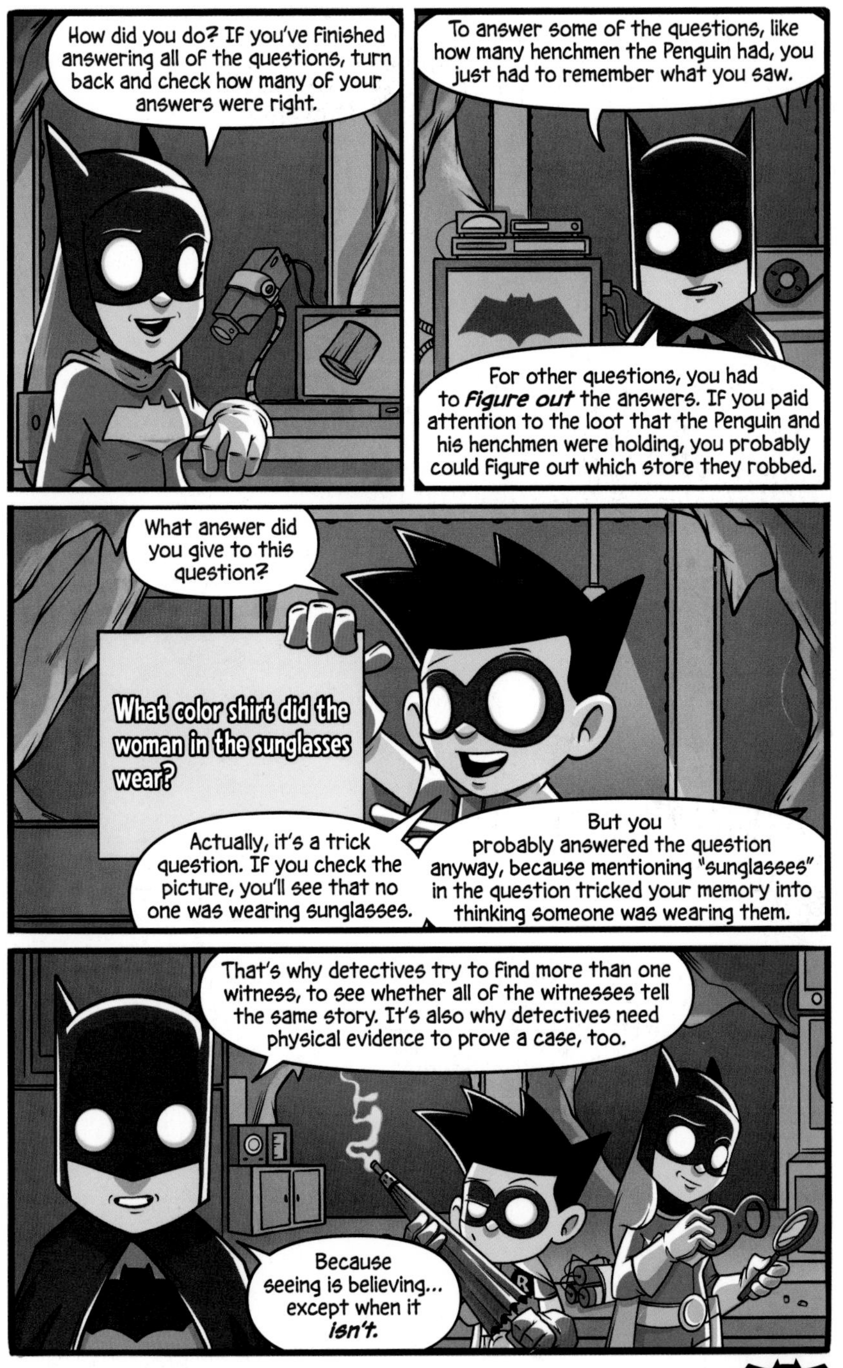
How did you do? If you've finished answering all of the questions, turn back and check how many of your answers were right.
To answer some of the questions, like how many henchmen the Penguin had, you just had to remember what you saw.
For other questions, you had to *figure out* the answers. If you paid attention to the loot that the Penguin and his henchmen were holding, you probably could figure out which store they robbed.
What answer did you give to this question?
What color shirt did the woman in the sunglasses wear?
Actually, it's a trick question. If you check the picture, you'll see that no one was wearing sunglasses.
But you probably answered the question anyway, because mentioning "sunglasses" in the question tricked your memory into thinking someone was wearing them.
That's why detectives try to find more than one witness, to see whether all of the witnesses tell the same story. It's also why detectives need physical evidence to prove a case, too.
Because seeing is believing... except when it *isn't.*

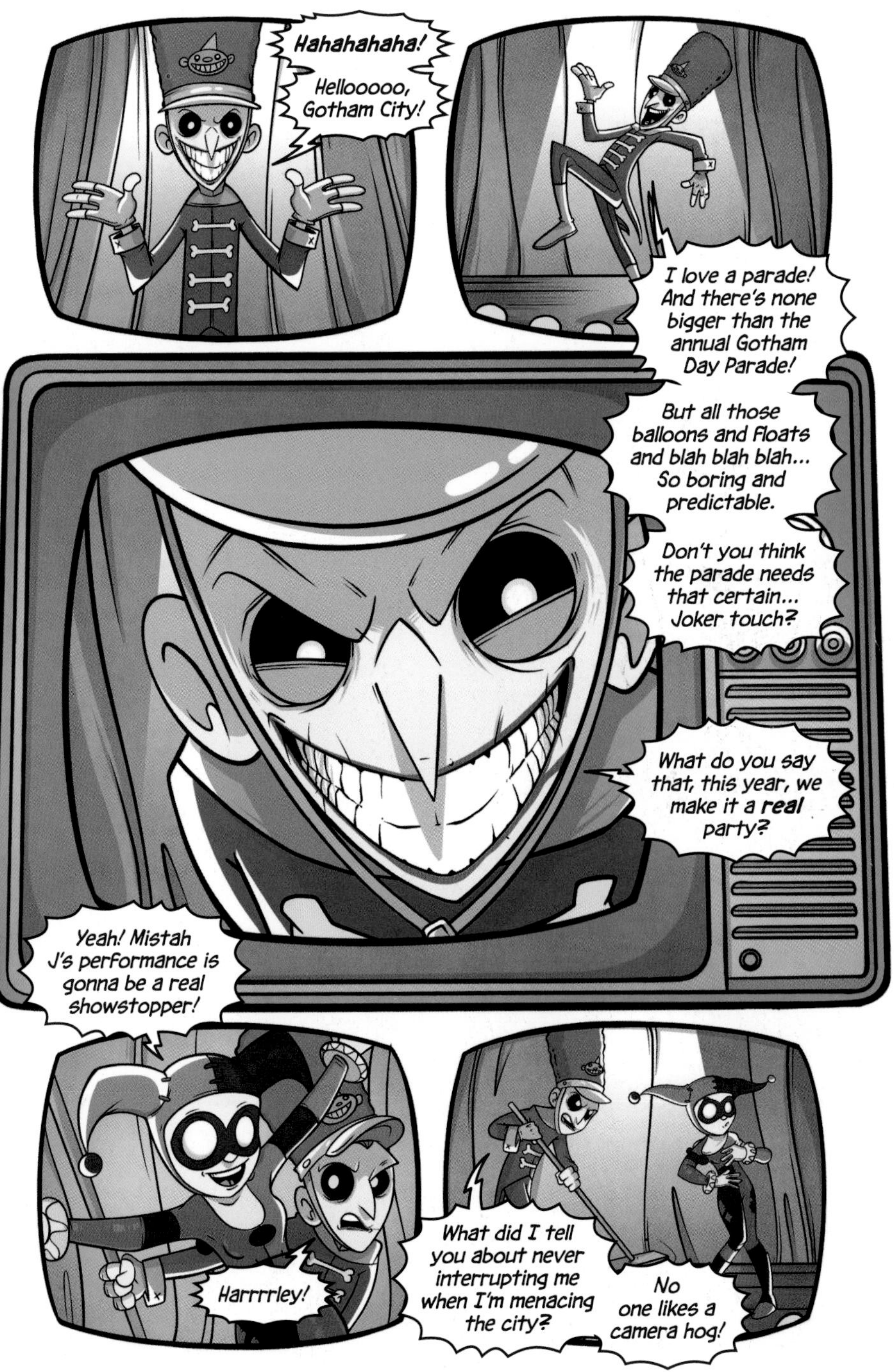
Hahahahaha!
Hellooooo, Gotham City!
I love a parade! And there's none bigger than the annual Gotham Day Parade!
But all those balloons and floats and blah blah blah... So boring and predictable.
Don't you think the parade needs that certain... Joker touch?
What do you say that, this year, we make it a **real** party?
Yeah! Mistah J's performance is gonna be a real showstopper!
Harrrrley!
What did I tell you about never interrupting me when I'm menacing the city?
No one likes a camera hog!

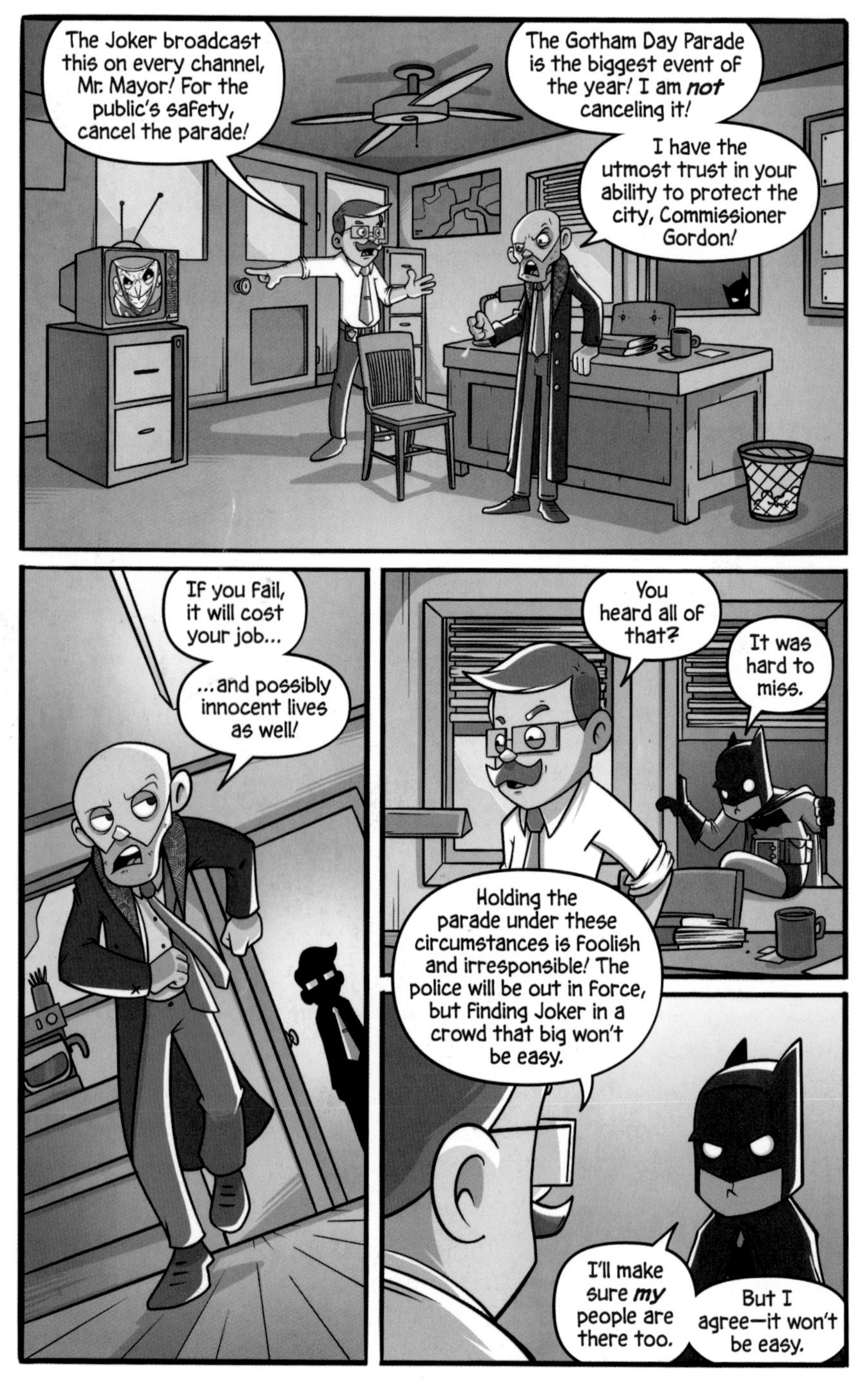
The Joker broadcast this on every channel, Mr. Mayor! For the public's safety, cancel the parade!
The Gotham Day Parade is the biggest event of the year! I am *not* canceling it!
I have the utmost trust in your ability to protect the city, Commissioner Gordon!
If you fail, it will cost your job...
...and possibly innocent lives as well!
You heard all of that?
It was hard to miss.
Holding the parade under these circumstances is foolish and irresponsible! The police will be out in force, but finding Joker in a crowd that big won't be easy.
I'll make sure *my* people are there too.
But I agree—it won't be easy.

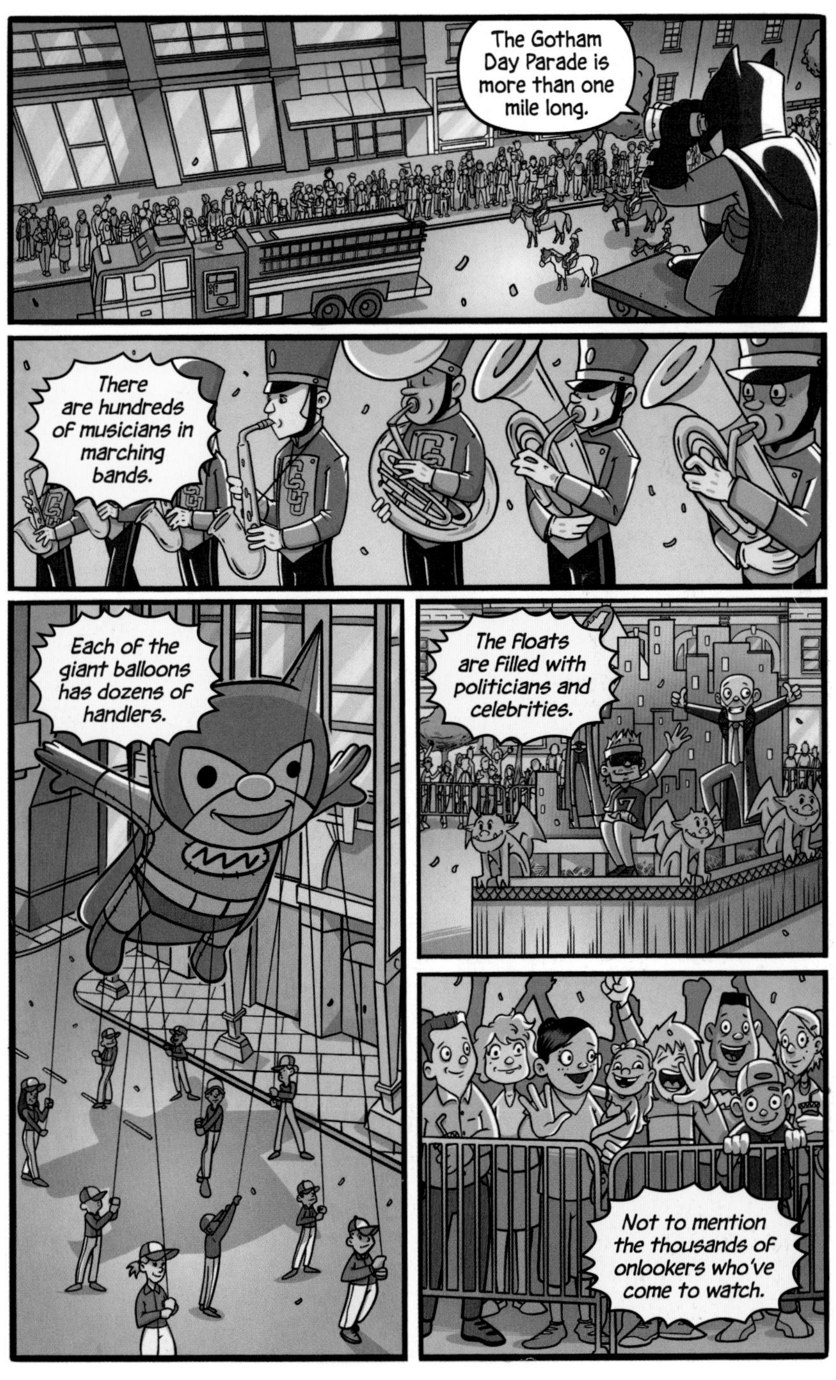
The Gotham Day Parade is more than one mile long.
There are hundreds of musicians in marching bands.
Each of the giant balloons has dozens of handlers.
The floats are filled with politicians and celebrities.
Not to mention the thousands of onlookers who've come to watch.

Chapter 7:
The Case of the Perilous Parade
Finding the Joker here is like looking for a needle in the world's biggest haystack.
ACME

Especially since he and Harley Quinn are sure to be disguised.

Everyone, check in. Batgirl?
Any sign of Joker activity at the north end of the parade?
Nothing yet.
It's a shame we can't just watch the parade, though.
Some of these performers are really impressive.
Maybe. But don't let your guard down.

Our top priority is keeping people safe!
Well, everything seems normal at the south end of the parade too. Listen for yourself.
KYTCHEN SYNC
Wow, Tad! Just when you think this parade can't get any better...
I know, Tammi! Our viewers at home are in for a treat, because here comes pop sensation Kytchen Sync performing their smash hit, "Can't Spell Unacceptable Without U"!
Girl, why'd you leave me, so lonely and so tired...
Like an old quart of milk that's already expired...
So far, I haven't seen anything more threatening than a boy band.
But I *am* keeping a particular eye out for ***clowns.***

Not a bad idea. Unfortunately...
There are a lot of clowns in this parade.
Of course, there's no guarantee that the Joker's dressed as a clown.
He could be anywhere in the parade, disguised as anything.

Indeed, sir. Nor is it necessarily the case that the Joker is among the parade's *marchers.*
That is precisely why I continue to search among the spectators.
Anyone unusual?
This is Gotham City, sir. *Everyone* is unusual.
However, I can't say I've encountered anyone who is obviously the Joker or Harley Quinn yet.
From the looks of things, it appears that the *police* haven't found them yet either.
104 ST. EXT
Can we be certain that the Joker and Ms. Quinn are even here?
Alfred has a point. The Joker and Harley could have sent *henchmen* to do their dirty work.

True, Batgirl. But that's unlikely.
The Joker enjoys his own cleverness too much. He'd want to see the chaos he causes in person.
Still, that doesn't narrow it down much.
But **where?** There are too many possibilities.
Instead of looking at each individual person, we need to look for patterns.
We need to find the thing that's out of place. The thing that's different.

Of course!
I know what breaks the pattern!
Attention, everyone! I think I've found the Joker!
Everyone converge on this location...
STOP!
DON'T TURN THE PAGE!
?
What clue did Batman find? Where are the Joker and Harley Quinn?
When you think you've found them, turn the page to see if you're right.

Keeping a giant helium balloon under control isn't easy. Each balloon in the parade is held down by a large crew of handlers.
So why is *this* giant balloon the only one that's tied down to a float instead?
Maybe because it's *not* filled with helium...
...but with Joker gas!
Stepping on my punch lines *again,* Batman? Didn't anyone ever tell you the secret to comedy is timing?
Not to mention knowin' when to get off the stage! Bye, now!
I was going to wait until we reached the grandstand before flooding Gotham with deadly gas.
But now, my gas will have to put a smile on the city from right here!

My gift to you, Gotham City! With love and kisses from the Jo—
WHUMMMMMPP
—kerrrr!
The city doesn't need your "gifts," Joker! And this one will never be delivered!
All we have to do is get the balloon far away from people—and far away from *you!*
Hahahaha! *Bat*-ter think twice, Batman!
You'll never carry that balloon far enough away before I trigger it with my remote control!
Two mistakes, Joker!
One: who said you're going to have your remote control?
KRUNNNCHH
And two: who said Batman was going to *carry* the balloon away?

Yeesh! Some people just can't take a joke!
But once I'm in that crowd, I can still blend in and get away!
Seriously? I know you like to dress up like a jester, but are you kidding?
If you want to blend in, you shouldn't wear clown makeup!
Urrrk!
And if you want to get away...
You shouldn't wear a wedding gown with a long train!
Oof!
Why, I oughta...
Uh, stay right here.
I oughta stay right here.
Hiya, Fellas. Anybody got gum?
Nice work, Batgirl! I couldn't be prouder if you were my own daughter!
Um... thanks...

This parade sure puts on a show! You'd almost think that's the *real* Batman and Joker!
It's over, Joker!
Not without an encore, Batman! Come a little closer!
Close enough to spray you with acid from my squirting flower—
Wh-?
Whooooopssss!
Ugh. I should've known you'd use some Bat-gizmo to trip me up.
What was it this time? Bat-hook? Bat-rolling pin? Invisible Bat-drone?
No, an even more effective secret weapon.
Quite right. One never knows when a sturdy umbrella might come in handy.
CASE CLOSED!

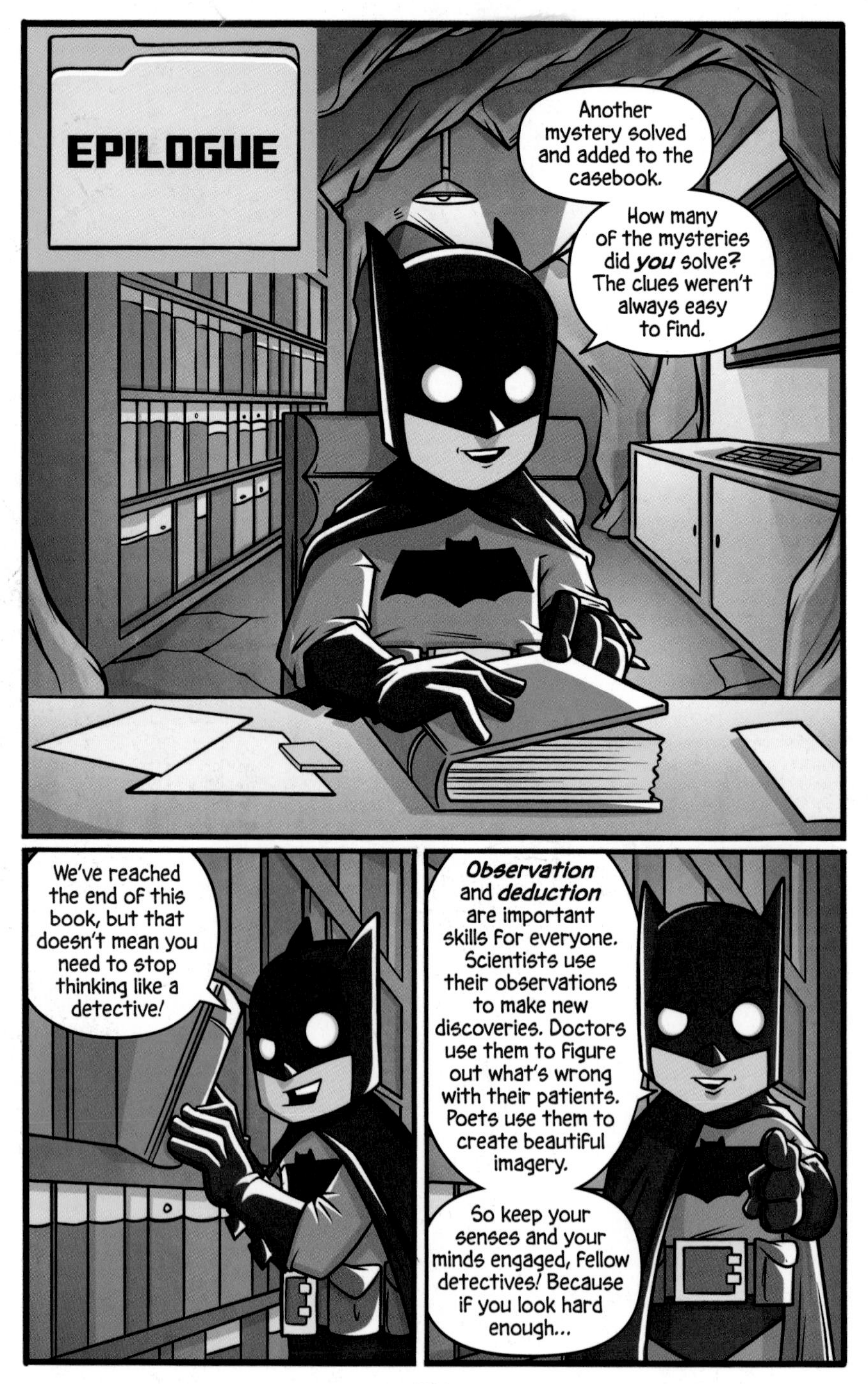
EPILOGUE
Another mystery solved and added to the casebook.
How many of the mysteries did *you* solve? The clues weren't always easy to find.
We've reached the end of this book, but that doesn't mean you need to stop thinking like a detective!
Observation and *deduction* are important skills for everyone. Scientists use their observations to make new discoveries. Doctors use them to figure out what's wrong with their patients. Poets use them to create beautiful imagery.
So keep your senses and your minds engaged, fellow detectives! Because if you look hard enough...

You'll find that the world is *full* of mystery!

SHOLLY FISCH is a mild-mannered developmental psychologist who has helped produce dozens of educational TV series, digital games, magazines, and hands-on materials, including *Sesame Street*, *Cyberchase*, *The Magic School Bus Rides Again*, *The Cat in the Hat Knows a Lot About That!*, and lots of things you've probably never heard of. He's spent more than 30 years writing everything from Superman to *Star Wars* to Scooby-Doo. His lovely wife, Susan, and brilliantly talented children, Nachum, Naomi, Chana, and Miriam, all hope he'll get more sleep someday.

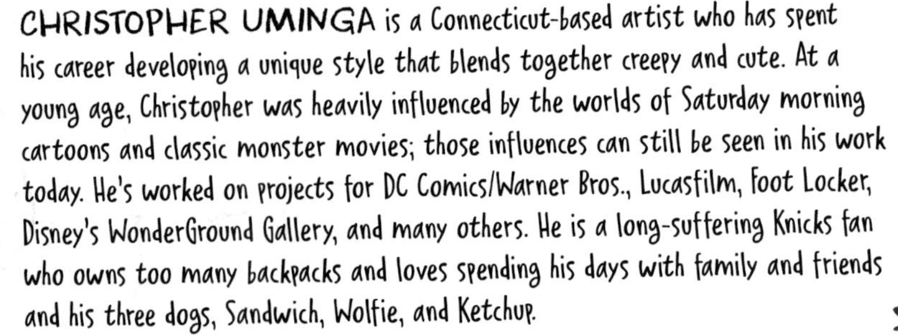

CHRISTOPHER UMINGA is a Connecticut-based artist who has spent his career developing a unique style that blends together creepy and cute. At a young age, Christopher was heavily influenced by the worlds of Saturday morning cartoons and classic monster movies; those influences can still be seen in his work today. He's worked on projects for DC Comics/Warner Bros., Lucasfilm, Foot Locker, Disney's WonderGround Gallery, and many others. He is a long-suffering Knicks fan who owns too many backpacks and loves spending his days with family and friends and his three dogs, Sandwich, Wolfie, and Ketchup.

SILVANA BRYS is a colorist and graphic designer who has colored *Scooby-Doo, Where Are You?*, *Teen Titans Go!*, *Scooby-Doo Team-Up*, and *Looney Tunes* for DC Comics, plus *Tom and Jerry* and many other comics and books. She lives in a small village in Argentina. Her home is also her office and she loves to create there, surrounded by forests and mountains.

ANDWORLD DESIGN is the super lettering team-up of Morgan Martinez, Justin Birch, and Deron Bennett. Together, they have created sound effects and word balloons for hundreds of comics just like the one you're reading now. Some of their favorite characters to work on have been Wonder Woman, Aquaman, and of course, Batman! Still kids at heart, they enjoy playing video games, collecting action figures, and meeting up with friends for thrilling board game sessions. Although they live in different parts of the country—Deron is in New Jersey, Morgan lives in New York, and Justin is from West Virginia—they still find time to get together when they can and chat regularly online.

I really love how you captured the cafeteria worker's expression! It's like everything is fine even though they're serving up toxic waste from a chemical factory that could turn you into a super-villain.

ice cream
MON AMOUR

Although, come to think of it, I don't know that any of Gotham's super-villains got their start that way. I'm sure they ended up doing bad deeds because they lacked love or resources or positive influences in their lives.

I kind of dig Penguin's fashion sense, but I sometimes feel bad for thinking that because, you know, crime.

What do you think of Killer Croc?

I don't know much about him other than he's a mean guy who steals from people.
Maybe he has to steal. Because of that stuff you said, not having, um...good friends or people that care about him.
It sounds like *you've* thought a lot about Killer Croc.
You're right. Maybe he hasn't had a fair life. But a lot of people haven't. We all make choices. That guy keeps making bad ones.

Hey there.
Hi, guys!
Andy, have you met my friends Ross, Jordan, and Josh?
Yeah. They made quite an impression.
Mind if we join you?
You can take my seat. I'd better be going.
We didn't finish the comic yet.
Give that back!
SWIPE
I can draw better than this, Maggie. You and I should work together.
You draw, Ross? How come you never show us your stuff?
Wow, that's actually really good, Andy!

I guess your drawing skills are okay.
Shame you can't draw yourself a new face, huh?
I know how I could improve your face.
SPLAT

After him!

It's not completely ruined.
Maybe the ice cream stain can work as the toxic waste?

We lost him.
Maybe we should head home now?

He's around here somewhere.

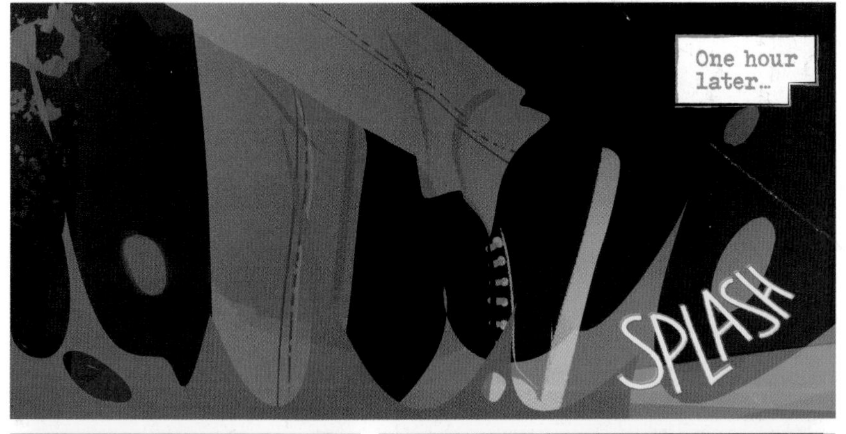
One hour later...
SPLASH

Get.
Out.